T0153111

Family ISSUE

by

Nat Burns

Bella
BOOKS

2014

Copyright © 2014 by Nat Burns

Bella Books, Inc.
P.O. Box 10543
Tallahassee, FL 32302

All rights reserved. No part of this book may be reproduced or transmitted in any form or by any means, electronic or mechanical, including photocopying, without permission in writing from the publisher.

Printed in the United States of America on acid-free paper.

First Bella Books Edition 2014

Editor: Medora MacDougall
Cover Designer: Judith Fellows

ISBN: 978-1-59493-378-3

PUBLISHER'S NOTE

The scanning, uploading, and distribution of this book via the Internet or via any other means without the permission of the publisher is illegal and punishable by law. Please purchase only authorized electronic editions, and do not participate in or encourage electronic piracy of copyrighted materials. Your support of the author's rights is appreciated.

Other Books by Nat Burns

House of Cards
Identity
Poison Flowers
The Book of Eleanor
The Quality of Blue
Two Weeks in August

Acknowledgements

I'd like to thank the southern half of the United States for being the unique and fascinating entity you are. I truly love to set my books in Southern locales because of the endless fascination and inspiration you provide.

Thanks also to my wonderful editor, Medora MacDougall. Her sense of humor accompanies her wise corrections and I actually look forward to her edits on my manuscripts. I know—how strange is that?

As always, tons of gratitude to Bella Books for publishing my flights of fancy and to you, dear readers, for remaining faithful and appreciative. It means a lot.

About the Author

Nat Burns is:

- A Goldie award-winning novelist with Bella Books
- An author with Regal Crest Enterprises
- A book editor with several publishers
- A music editor with a monthly magazine column, Notes from Nat.
- A previous board member of the Small Press Writers and Artists Organization, the Nelson County Education Foundation, Literacy Volunteers of America and the Golden Crown Literary Society.
- A retired journalist, software technician and editorial systems coordinator who has lived in Virginia, South Texas and now New Mexico.

www.natburns.com
www.facebook.com/natburnsworld
@NattyBurns

I'd like to dedicate this book to the family and friends who devotedly buoy me up when the times get rough. Thank you. Much love to you.

CHAPTER ONE

"I'm sorry, Mr. Anderson. You should have thought of that before you went bungee jumping with your friends while you were vacationing at Virginia Beach."

I shifted the phone headset, then listened absently, gently rolling the wooden cylinder of a yellow pencil back and forth across the pitted maple desktop. And I sighed, bored with the worn, familiar song I was hearing. I studied my drab office walls, thinking once again that I needed to get a mural of some sort. Or, at the very least, a movie poster.

"I know, Mr. Anderson. I know. But you are supposed to be suffering the effects of whiplash. And I can't find the physician you listed either. The one who you said would support your claims. We absolutely have to deny it."

I paused as I fished a second pencil from the pencil cup and added it to the first. The gentle susurrus of controlled sound was a comforting counterpoint to the angry shouting coming from the phone headset. I closed my eyes, wishing I had stayed home in bed that morning.

"Yes, it is a lot of money. And my name is Denni, sir, Denni Hope. You can report me to whomever you please, but calling me those kinds of names won't help you get approved."

I cringed as a new volley of angry words assailed me. "Mr. Anderson. Mr. Anderson? I am ending this conversation now. If you wish to take it up with our legal representation, the contact information is at the bottom of the email and the hard copy letter that I have just sent to you. The email and letter will explain in detail why the claim was denied and all about the appeal process. Goodbye, sir."

Taking a deep breath, I sat back in my chair and stared through the large plate glass window on the south wall of my office, watching the pedestrians moving busily on the street outside. The office work—with its ensuing confrontations—was my least favorite aspect of this job. Eyeing the desk in my peripheral vision, I grimaced at the four folders awaiting action. I was simply not in the mood to work. Period.

The on-the-fly sleuthing was the fun part, anyway, catching people in lies and deceptions. Plus the research and fact-checking, the work of coolly building a case against someone trying to steal from Alan Carter's insurance company. But taking this kind of abuse for something the client did to himself...well, it was not fun. I glanced at the waiting folders and sighed again.

I knew I needed to get on with it, but my thoughts kept drifting to the real issue bothering me. I couldn't shake the troubling nature of Patty's call. I'd come back from lunch, and her message had been there waiting for me, a voice mail heralded by a red blinking light on my blocky office phone.

Examining my feelings with some wonder, I tried to put aside the warm waves engendered in my body upon hearing Patty's voice again, even on an answering machine. Yet I was alarmed to hear a panicked note, one that I'd never heard in the five years we'd been together as a couple.

My fingers crept back to the pencils on the desktop. I studied the two rolling cylinders with a pensive gaze. Should I go? The panic in Patty's tone frightened me. This was the troubling issue, not so much the destruction of Patty's possessions or the fact that someone seemed to be hounding her. These problems could be dealt with, were dealt with every day in my line of work. It was that small tremble in Patty's voice that haunted me. That tiny clue that let me know just how close Patty was to losing it.

Even more troubling was the feeling Patty's distress provoked in me. No matter how I tried to demonize Patty because she had heartlessly left me for another, the powerful love I'd felt for her lingered. And now she needed me.

A looped-together line of preschool-aged children passed by the window and I watched their undeniable cuteness with brooding eyes.

Should I go to Louisiana and help Patty? Immerse myself anew in her world, even temporarily? Could my emotions handle the pain of being within touching distance yet not able to touch? I sat back and slowly rocked back and forth in my soft desk chair, soothing myself as my thoughts tussled like misbehaving youngsters. A huge part of me wanted to ignore or deny the plea, while the smaller, gentler side of me very badly needed to help her.

Do we ever truly get over those we have loved?

I absently pulled the headset from my head. Dew dripped from the rooftop above the window and arced in a sudden gust of wind, sparkling a brief farewell to the brilliant Virginia sunlight before merging with the shaded darkness of the sidewalk below. I took a deep breath and decided the sparkle was a good sign, an omen of full speed ahead.

I spun away from the window and stared at the thick glass door that led into the shadowy confines of the Carter Insurance Company's main office. I saw Macy Logan, our attractive secretary extraordinaire, hunched over a keyboard busily typing. My thoughts rambled through the few short-term relationships I had been involved in since Patty. Perhaps if one of them had stuck, had become long term, I might have gotten over Patty completely by now.

"I still cannot believe he did that." Tom Miles's form suddenly filled the doorway. I knew exactly which case he was talking about. The bungee jumper. "It's amazing what people think they can get away with…just boggles the mind," he continued.

I studied him. Short and balding, he was wearing his habitual crisp business suit, his face ruddy above the tight collar of his button-down Oxford shirt and red striped tie. "I know. And he really thought he could get away with it. I finally sent him over to Legal."

"I guess they think no one is watching." Tom's smile was crafty.

I smiled. "You'd think with hundreds of thousands of dollars at stake, he'd assume we'd be checking him out. I mean, we're not just gonna give it to him, for chrissakes."

"Do you think he's gonna drag Legal into it?" He plopped down into the chair on the opposite side of my desk. He stared out the window behind me, his mind obviously whirring with thought.

I leaned back and nodded. "Probably. He doesn't have a leg to stand on, though."

"Still, it costs beyond the retainer."

He finally looked directly at me, and I suddenly made up my mind.

"Listen, Tom…I was thinking about taking a little time off…"

He leaned forward and studied my face. "It's about time."

This wasn't the response I was expecting. "What do you mean?"

"You've only taken sick time during the past several years, no vacation time at all. You're long overdue." He blinked slowly.

I sat silently thinking a few minutes, and I realized that what he said was true. I'd been so busy trying to immerse myself in my work so I wouldn't think about the breakup that I had given up on any life beyond work. I let out a deep breath.

"How long were you thinking?"

I stared down at my desk calendar and saw a pretty much empty schedule. "How's a week sound?"

Tom stood and smiled at me. "It sounds perfect. I'll let Alan know. Will you clear everything with Macy?"

I nodded and indicated the folders on my desk. "I'll wrap these up too, before I go."

"Good. So what do you have planned?" He paused by the doorway on his way out.

I shrugged. "I think I'll head down south and visit some friends. Nothing fancy."

Tom nodded and moved down the hall, waving over his shoulder. "Have a good time! And if you can't be good, just don't get caught!"

His laughter wafted to me as his office door slid shut.

I took a deep breath and picked up the phone headset. It was time to get back to work. I felt a great sense of relief...and trepidation...now that the decision had been made.

DAY ONE

CHAPTER TWO

John Clyde Price was waiting for me at the little Lake Charles, Louisiana, airport when I got in at four that Sunday evening. I had changed planes twice—a long flight very early that morning from Virginia to New Orleans, then a quick hop over to Lake Charles. Unable to relax, I had tried reading during both legs of the flight but had eventually drifted into a fitful doze. I was oddly nervous about returning to the area where Patty and I had lived. Where we had loved. I wasn't sure how I would be received, especially by Yolanda, the woman Patty had left me for.

Patty's brother had changed little during the four years since I'd last seen him. A tall, lanky man, he reminded me of Abraham Lincoln, even down to the untamed shock of dark hair. He was not nearly as rough in feature, though. His face actually resembled Patty's in some small ways, and she was one of the loveliest women I had ever known. His smile was infectious, full of overlarge white teeth and shy, flirtatious charm.

"It's good to see you, John Clyde. It's been a while." I let my eyes roam across his features with true fondness. We'd shared a number of good times hanging out at Bay Sally's Bar, fishing lines in the water, beers warming between our thighs. He'd been a good ear when Patty and I started having trouble. No judgment, just quiet comfort.

"Denni," he said, nodding his head in welcome. "It's good to see you again." I did notice that he'd grown thinner and there were dark circles around his eyes. His hair had begun to gray a little, mostly at the temples.

"So, what's the deal? What do you think is going on here?" As was my wont, I got right to the point.

He sighed as he lifted my duffel into the bed of the sleek double cab pickup truck he was driving. License plates with the name of the family business, Fortune Farm, revealed that it was not his private vehicle. A good thing as the last car I'd remembered him owning had been a tiny foreign something that had barely held his own long legs much less a solid one hundred seventy pounds of insurance investigator.

"I don't know, Denni gal. You know Mama died in the spring. Brain rupture just took her overnight."

"I know. And I'm so, so sorry. You know I'm gonna miss Megs. She was like a mother to me too."

If I hadn't been looking so keenly—or if my eyes hadn't been so professionally attuned to such cues, I might have missed it. There was a sudden subtle tautening of the skin around his mouth and eyes. What had been grief, the next minute was… what? Perhaps grief still.

"I wish y'all had let me know then. I would have liked to have come down and pay my respects," I said quietly.

"Well, we were all fit to be tied. I thought Patty was gonna die right along with Mama." He looked away and I felt my heart lurch in sad empathy. "That's when it started."

"What started?"

He screwed his face into a tight frown as he headed the truck west. "First it was things disappearing from Mama's room. Things Patty had wanted to keep, like Mama's jewelry. Then it was the tractors. The whole fleet. Someone sugared the tanks. Cost us thousands to get them fixed."

I let loose a low whistle. Destructive behavior at its finest. "When was this?"

"I guess about a month or so after Mama passed."

I studied the scenery as John Clyde eased the truck onto the access road that emptied onto Main Street. Lake Charles, Louisiana, had not changed much in the handful of years since I'd last been there. It was a sprawling town of hotels, restaurants and casinos. We passed through the snug little heart of downtown on our way to Route 171 south toward Brethren and I studied the people dotting the sidewalks. They looked the same as always—the natives tired and threadbare and the tourists' faces filled with hope and a surety that they would win at the gaming tables. I saw where several long-standing mom-and-pop businesses had been ravaged by storms and also noted many more casinos than had been there four years ago.

The historic Virginia town I lived in now seemed much more affluent, the residents more polished, more metropolitan. I had forgotten how unrelenting poverty and the desperation of subsistence living could age people. But Cameron Parish was a scrapper. In 1957, Hurricane Audrey had come through and brutally wiped out most of the town's residences and outlying businesses. The people rebuilt right away, but in 2005, Hurricane Rita paid a lingering visit and laughed at what they'd accomplished. By the time Hurricane Isaac came to visit in 2008, there was little structure or spirit left in Louisiana's most westward parish. From what John Clyde was telling me, farms were still limping along these days and more businesses were now closed than open.

As we passed through the small downtown area, I saw some of that remaining futility in the faces of the residents. But I also saw that enduring charm that is possessed by those residing in small southern towns—a charm that isn't often found in many, more urban, places, even certain cities in Virginia. Some people where I lived now were downright snooty. I knew these people here really would give you the shirt off their back, even if it meant their own skin was left to deal with the elements. I readily returned the warm smiles I received from curious passersby as the truck paused at a stoplight.

"What happened next?" I reluctantly pulled my gaze from a cherubic toddler trying in vain to keep up with an older brother.

John Clyde grasped the steering wheel with both hands, hard, until his knuckles faded to white. "Little things mostly. Then Kissy went missing."

"Kissy?"

"Patty and Yolanda's daughter."

"They have a daughter?" A strange feeling stirred below my breastbone.

"Yeah, a four-year-old, adopted formally about six months ago."

"Oh. Patty never told me. What happened to her? Is she okay?"

"Yes." He nodded thoughtfully as he watched the road. "She was missing for several hours, and we had the whole farm looking for her. She turned up wandering the banks of Ruddy Bayou."

"Well, what happened? Did she get lost? How did she get away from the house by herself?"

"It appears that someone whacked her on the head from behind and then threw her in the water to be eaten by gators. Luckily the water revived her and she made it to the side. Thank goodness Patty and Landa insisted on those swimming lessons last summer."

"I just don't get it," I said, studying the side of John Clyde's face as though the answers resided there. "Why would someone want to hurt the little girl? That makes no sense."

"I think to get at Patty, or maybe Yolanda," John Clyde mused. We were some miles south of town now, and he slowed to take the right onto Route 171, which would take us farther south to Pepperwood Trail and Fortune Farm.

Wide green road signs proclaimed that we were now bypassing Brethren, Louisiana, home of the Flathead Catfish. Brethren, population just under one thousand, was a small, sleepy community set along the Sabine River. The main employer for the area was the hospital, named after lumber baron slash philanthropist, Ernest Glass, then the ConAgra factory and then the Gulf Oil refinery on the banks of Sabine Lake.

It was a tourist's paradise, however, and people flocked to hotels and restaurants on the outskirts of Brethren to fish or ski Sabine Lake or to save money as they played the gaming tables in Lake Charles. Hell, a lot of the residents commuted the half hour's drive into Lake Charles for jobs where the easy money was just that much sweeter.

I lowered my eyes from the boring highway scenery and thought about the things that had been happening. I wondered who Patty, John Clyde or Yolanda could have angered to such an extent. The Price family was one of the more well-connected and prosperous farming families and had garnered a good share of community respect.

"Do you think it is a lifestyle issue?" I asked finally. "Like those women over in Ovett, Mississippi, who found dead animals hanging on their mailbox?"

"Maybe," he replied, studying me briefly. "The people around here all pretty much know about Patty and don't seem to care." He colored slightly. "I mean, you and Patty never had any trouble when you were together, did you?"

When we were together. I allowed the memory of those days to overtake me. I usually avoided thinking about Patty and the way we had loved one another and was surprised now to discover the pain had finally lessened somewhat.

A shrill sound fractured the silence that had grown between us. John Clyde reached between the truck seats and fetched the ringing phone that was plugged into the dash.

"John Clyde Price," he said after he flipped open the small, clamshell-styled phone. He listened a moment. "Goddamn," he replied finally. "We're almost there."

"Who was it?" I asked, worried by the grimness of John Clyde's face after he closed the phone. This was a new face, one I'd never seen on him before. He was an affable man, generally, prone to laughter and pranks. This new, angry man was a stranger.

"It was Paul. They got the goats."

"The goats?" I repeated, feeling stupid.

"Patty's baby goats. She was raising goats for cheese and to sell, but she couldn't let go of the babies. Fell in love with them." He lowered his foot on the gas pedal and restlessly guided the truck toward home. I felt a sour stirring in the center of my gut.

"What happened to them?"

"They're dying."

CHAPTER THREE

Human, the Labrador mutt Patty and I had rescued from the animal shelter seven years ago, greeted the truck with a subdued trot as we passed through the white wooden wing gates of Fortune Farm. Slowly bypassing the sprawling white farmhouse, John Clyde pulled the truck around to the edge of the landscaped backyard, where a large fenced-in lot had been set up for the goats. Several farmhands had crowded around the tall, chain-link entry, but they moved aside quickly to let John Clyde and me through. One of the older hands, a man named Real, balding and distinguished, though smudged with rich, black Louisiana dirt, was gently trying to pull Patty away from the randomly scattered, fallen goats.

"Come on, miss, you just let us handle this now," he said, his somber, soothing voice carrying to me and causing sudden tears to sprout in my eyes.

Patty allowed herself to be led to the gate, where her gaze fell on me. Then she was in my arms, her body convulsing as she sobbed her grief into the front of my T-shirt. I, momentarily taken aback, found memory the oarsman that guided my hands to Patty's back, found an old voice that calmed the child in Patty. I lowered my face, permitting myself the luxury of closing my eyes and experiencing the welcome fit of Patty in my arms. John Clyde moved close to pass by both of us, and I suddenly remembered the here and now.

Opening my eyes, I saw Yolanda watching with a cool, shuttered expression as the eight or so farmhands followed John Clyde and moved past us to carry away the tiny carcasses.

Yolanda Elliott had changed little in the years since she'd stolen Patty from me. She was still tall and slender, with blond, spiky hair, cropped very short. Her face was pleasant, but often vacant, and after the breakup, I had often wondered what had drawn Patty so forcibly to her. The few times I had swallowed my pride and actually tried to talk with Yolanda had been surprising disappointments; Yolanda seemed to lack even the most fundamental of conversational skills. Or maybe she just plain didn't like me. We certainly had nothing in common. Except Patty.

"I just can't believe someone would do this to helpless animals!" Patty had pulled back and was watching the removal operation with sorrow, occasionally sobbing with an intake of breath. Human pressed himself against her thighs, clearly distressed by her anguish.

"Well, what happened?" John Clyde asked petulantly, running fingers through his already tousled hair. He looked bewildered.

Patty shook her head. "I can't say, John Clyde. Paul came in the back door and asked me to come have a look because the goats were acting funny, like they were drugged or something. By the time Landa and I got out here Peaches was already gone."

Her face contorted with the memory, and I automatically grasped her shoulder to reassure and calm her.

"Did anyone see someone strange hanging around the pen today?" I asked, studying the rapidly diminishing crowd of farm workers.

"I already asked Real, and he said no one noticed anything unusual. The regular crew fed and watered them and about a half hour later they started stumbling," Yolanda said, as she stepped forward and extended her hand to me for a cursory handshake. There was a nod of acknowledgment, maybe truce, and we both turned our focus back toward Patty.

"Have you noticed anyone, or anything, unusual on the ranch, Patty?" I asked.

Patty sighed heavily to express her exasperation. "No, Denni, no one, nothing. Just the vandalism. I really hope you can get to the bottom of this, otherwise I'm gonna lose my mind, for sure."

CHAPTER FOUR

Seeing Patty's growing distress, John Clyde and I exchanged a pointed glance and began herding Patty and Yolanda toward the back door. Entering the bright, spacious kitchen, I realized I fully expected Megs's cheery welcome and motherly bustling. The lack was keenly felt.

"I'll get tea," Yolanda said as she approached the sink. "Y'all go into the sitting room where it's cool."

Before I passed into the interior of the house, my eyes drank in the familiar and some new, unfamiliar details. There seemed to be little that had changed overall. Much was as I remembered from those holiday family gatherings during the years Patty and I had been together. The kitchen was big and brightly lit from many large, strategically placed windows. The work areas had been modernized, with long lengths of counter interspersed with a deep sink and a stovetop, while a plethora of cabinets and a dishwasher rested below. The floor plan was open and two refrigerators towered on either side of the counters. It was spotless and I knew that it was from their lifelong housekeeper Ammie's meticulous ways.

It did smell differently, however. The heavy lavender scent favored by Megs had been replaced by a lighter citrus fragrance, no doubt from modern plug-in air fresheners.

I walked from the kitchen into the dining room with its large oval table and thick, heavy chairs. Age-darkened maple wainscoting separated the lower walls from pretty silk-striped wallpaper in muted tones of green and burgundy. There were no windows in this room but a lovely maple sideboard, laden with silver, provided a pleasant visual experience. The far wall bore a glass-fronted china cabinet that I knew had been in Megs's family for centuries. Delicate china, discolored from much use, cluttered the shelves inside. The glass on the cabinet was so old that it was warped and waved like a fun house mirror.

We passed through and on the other side of the dining room, across a short entry hall, we entered a large sitting room, furnished with a huge Oriental rug, two sofas set at ninety degrees and two easy chairs and a coffee table cradled within them for a comfortable conversation area. The front wall of the room featured a huge panoramic window that looked out over the Price cropland.

John Clyde settled Patty, with muttered assurances, into a corner of one of the heavily padded sofas, then moved to the back wall of the paneled room. The entire wall was an elaborate bar setup, with a polished wooden sideboard and long shelves lined with liquor bottles.

"Tea just ain't gonna do it for me," he announced to the room. "I need something a little bit stronger. Anyone else?"

I shook my head and Patty remained silent, so John Clyde shrugged and poured himself a healthy shot of scotch. Single malt, I noted with absurd clarity.

"Patty, are you going to be all right?" I moved to sit across from Patty on the other cushion-filled sofa. I leaned forward so I could see her face.

Patty lifted eyes filled with frustration. "I suppose I'll have to be. It's all so wrong, though. Know what I mean?"

"I know, hon, I know. What do you think is going on here? You didn't really specify a lot on the phone, just said that someone was trying to hurt the family. I don't understand what that means. Do you have any idea who it is?" I lifted one hand and crumpled my hair in frustration.

Patty shifted to one side and stared at my shoes. "Everything was okay until Mama died. We had the funeral and people came from just everywhere to pay their last respects. She was cremated and put into Little John's and life went on. We were grieving but getting on with things."

She lifted her gaze. "Then I got a call. From Little John. Someone, some bastard, had gone over to the mortuary and defaced her crypt."

"Defaced? Defaced how?" I looked over at John Clyde, wondering why he hadn't mentioned this. His gaze was elsewhere, his attention on the other side of the big bay window that dominated the sitting room.

"Well, the flowers were all broken and scattered, and someone had written LIAR across the front of the identification plate. Right there in front for everyone to see." Patty's voice hitched as sobs threatened to return.

"Don't forget BITCH," John Clyde offered dully. He was now watching Patty with vacant eyes.

"'Bitch'?" I asked.

Patty nodded. "That too. It was written on the marble below. It took me and Landa a whole afternoon to scrub it all off."

I sighed. "And then what happened?"

"Someone dumped sugar in the tractors and we had to clean and replace all the tanks and filters. It was awful. And no one saw anybody do it, which is weird," Patty replied. "You know how many people are here on this farm."

"It was during the night, about a week or so later," John Clyde explained.

I nodded. "And then your little girl was hurt?"

"Yes." Patty sat up straighter and her eyes flashed with fury. "Some son of a bitch hit her with something from behind, smacking her right into the bayou. I was looking for her, because she had wandered off, and I get down there by the bayou and see her walking toward me, blood running all down her face and neck..." She shuddered at the memory. "I will kill whoever did it, if I'm given half the chance."

"Here we go," Yolanda said as she entered the room. "I fixed Earl Grey. Hope that's okay with everyone." She placed the tray on the coffee table and sat next to Patty.

"How are you holding up?" she asked softly.

Patty's expression eased as she smiled at Yolanda, and I was struck by the rightness of their relationship. Old tensions unwound just a little as I finally found a way to accept that fact.

Yolanda poured steaming cups of tea and passed them around.

"Yolanda, can you think of anyone who would want to do this?" I asked. I took a tentative sip and felt unusually fortified by the strong, fragrant brew.

"What? You mean kill the goats? Trash the tractors and push our baby into the bayou? No, no one comes to mind. I can't imagine anyone being so vicious."

"Patty? I mean if you *had* to guess someone."

"No, no one. The poor goats had to have been poisoned and that means access to their food. Or water. We'll have to test both of them and...and do an autopsy on one of the... them."

"Why would someone poison them? It's crazy. Seems like someone wants to hurt you personally," I mused.

Patty sighed, pensive herself. "I've been tormenting myself about that. I can't imagine why anyone would want to be so heartless to me...to us."

"Could it have been someone angry with your mom? Or even your dad?" I asked.

"Maybe. But seems if that were so, John Clyde and I would remember some mention of it. We discussed that possibility early on, after the tractors, and neither of us can remember any suspicion of it when they were alive."

"She's right, everyone seemed to love Dodson and Megs and thought it well-deserved," John Clyde said. He was still standing at the bar, now idly stirring the amber liquid in his glass with an index finger.

I sat thoughtful for half a minute. "Any competition? Whose business might y'all be stepping on?"

"There's only one other producer close in this area and that's Taylor Morrissey," John Clyde replied.

Patty eyed her brother with a tolerant expression. "And you know Taylor would never allow this sort of crap to go on. He and Daddy were best of friends, had been just about forever. They even went to school together before Taylor moved away."

"Hell, I wouldn't put it past him," John Clyde disagreed. "When it comes to money, friendship is thin milk."

"John Clyde, why do you say such things, much less even think them?" Patty cried.

He laughed softly at her angry scowl, as if thinking it much better than the sadness of a moment ago. "Mainly 'cause they're true!" he replied.

I sat back. "Well, we'll have to investigate him. His competitor status definitely marks him as a suspect."

"Not necessarily," Patty countered. "It could be one of his hands or anyone who hates us. Hey, maybe it's Alejandro, our new hand. He scares me a little."

"Scares you? Why?" I leaned forward again, interested.

"I don't like the way he looks at me. It's like he knows something I don't. I don't think he likes women in power," she explained.

"Patty," John Clyde interjected, "there's a lot of people like that in the world. He's a good worker and I've had him checked out. You shouldn't judge before you know him better."

Patty ignored John Clyde. "I have no idea who's doing this. Why poison helpless goats? That has nothing to do with the hay or sugarcane business. I was going to sell the milk and the babies but decided to keep them as pets instead."

"It does appear to be a personal attack directed to you," I reiterated quietly.

John Clyde nodded his agreement and poured himself a second drink.

Patty rose and tugged the hem of her T-shirt. "I don't want to talk about this anymore. Those poor babies stumbling around like that. It just tears my heart open. John Clyde, I want you to get a sampling of that water and food and we'll take them over for testing first thing in the morning. Landa, has Ammie gotten back from the store?"

"Yeah, when I was making tea. She's working on dinner."

Patty smoothed her dark hair back from her face and smiled thinly at me. "Well, welcome, Miss Denni. Looks as though you got a big job ahead of you. Let me take you on into the guest room and get you settled. I'm afraid I'm not a very good host today."

"Believe me," I replied. "I won't hold it against you. It's perfectly understandable given the circumstances."

I rose and took one more lingering look around the room, reminiscing. "Let me get my bag. It's just outside."

CHAPTER FIVE

Moving back through the kitchen after stowing my bag in the guest room off the downstairs back hallway, I took advantage of an unusual opportunity—finding Ammie Mose standing in one place—and gently grabbed the waist of the woman who was peeling vegetables at the sink.

"Oh Lord, look what the cat done brought in," the elderly woman exclaimed as she spun and spied me. She pulled me into a long, hard hug. "It is so good to see you. Miss Patty said you were coming to help us. I don't know what you were thinking moving back up north like you did."

"It's nice there. I like my job too. Alan Carter's been good to me."

"But it's so cold up there, baby. You need to be down here where it's warm and all the people love you so much."

"Yeah, the people—and the bugs! I get eaten up every time I come down here. Look here." I held out an arm, showing where a small red mark had risen just above my wrist.

"Them skeeters, they love the sweet meat, don't they?" Ammie chuckled at her own joke as she pulled a pinch of tiny thyme leaves and a few smaller basil leaves from herb pots growing in the larger of the two kitchen windows. She mixed them with something from a bottle, something that smelled a little like vinegar, until the substance was a creamy paste. She rubbed a small bolus of the paste into my mosquito bite. "Don't scratch it now; you'll ruin the magic."

I laughed sadly. I had sorely missed Ammie's Cajun ways and healing prowess and hadn't realized it until this very moment. "You are a wonder, Ammie," I said quietly.

"I guess you heard about the disagreements going on in the area?" Ammie's voice was assuming yet informing.

"No," I took a seat at the small breakfast nook and helped myself to strawberries piled in a wicker basket. "What disagreements?" How I loved Ammie's interminable gossip.

"Oh, it's awful." Ammie was mixing eggs at the counter as she spoke, adding chopped broccoli and onion in small handfuls. "There's some that say the land hereabouts has the oil. Others say it's all a lie, brought by the developers to move us all out."

"Developers, here? What do they see in Brethren that we can't see?"

Ammie smiled indulgently. "They want the hotels, the swimming pools, the little golf game, all of that."

"Why here? You're not even on a good stretch of the water. That's ridiculous."

"That's why they say it's oil. They've been promising oil here since the forties, but there's no oil yet."

I cupped my chin in my palm. "Well, there is oil over near Grand Lake and that's only about, what? Fifty miles?"

"Yes, about that," Ammie agreed. She was pouring the quiche batter into a partially baked pie shell.

"I wonder if that has anything to do with what's going on here at Fortune," I mused.

"No, it's just bad luck that's come to visit here, that's all. Bad hoodoo."

I grimaced at Ammie, all the while noting the white that had piped through her long, onyx black hair. She still wore it the same as always, twisted into a smooth oval and fastened firmly to the back of her head. Her lovely Greek features had softened while I had been away, however, and a touch of middle-age spread had crept onto her once too-thin waistline. I wondered briefly how old Ammie really was; she seemed ageless and had been taking care of the Price family since before John Clyde was born.

"You don't believe that. What about Kissy being hit on the head and thrown into the swamp? Hoodoo didn't do that, people did."

Ammie covered her ears with her palms. "I won't hear about that. I just thank the Lord every day that she was able to come back to us."

"Ammie, why do you think this all started after Megs died?" I pulled the top off another strawberry.

The quiche safely in the oven, Ammie sat across from me and sipped from a sweating glass of iced water. "Beats all. Probably because if it had happened while she was alive it would have put her *into* her grave."

She watched me with calm brown eyes. "I know she would've liked to have laid eyes on you again before she went away. She talked about you a lot, child. She and that Yolanda never did get on."

I could have said I was not surprised but chose to remain silent.

"So you're going to find out who's trying to hurt my babies?"

"Yes, ma'am, I am. Who do you think it is, really? I know you've thought about it."

Ammie grew contemplative. "That's between the land and the Lord. I can't put a face to it though I've shaken my brain every which way," she said finally.

"No one? You have to have some ideas." I knew that in most cases of mayhem, the perpetrator was well known to the victim or the victim's families.

"Maybe Jimmy Thibideaux from across the way. I saw him one day. He was out back when I was spreading for the chickens one morning. Now why would he be out there at daybreak?"

I was intrigued. "What was he doing?"

"Just looking around. I watched him for some time without him knowin' I was there. He was snoopin' but I didn't see him do nothing."

"Nothing suspicious?"

"No. He was just lookin' stuff over like he was buyin.' I ask what he was doing there and he say he was walking for the exercise."

"Walking?"

Ammie nodded. "I say, humph, he can walk his own place. I say it like the joke, though, and he laugh and go on his way."

I frowned. Jimmy Thibideaux. I didn't remember much about him, other than the familiar name. "What do you know about him, Ammie?"

"Jimmy? His is one of the old families. The Thibideaux been here longer than my people. There's five of them kids, all told. You might remember Ron. He's the one owns Sprouse's Market, where we get all our fresh stuff."

"Ron. Is he the oldest?" I asked.

Ammie paused to sort memory. "No," she said finally. "I think it's Ernie, then come little Jilly, only big as a minute, then Ron. Elizabeth was next, and Jimmy was the baby of them all. Ernie passed, you know."

"No. When?"

"About a year ago. Summer."

"Why do you think Jimmy would harm the Prices?" I watched Ammie closely.

Ammie shifted and focused her eyes directly on mine. "I don't necessarily think it's so. I'm just talking out of hand. As far as I know, Jimmy's never hurt a fly, nor would."

I nodded my acceptance. "What about his father, Thomas?"

"Thomas, now he was a good man. But loved the ladies, he did. Dona wasn't cold in her grave before he took up with that Baby Wood. She was good enough, I guess, and bless her for putting up with his cheating ways. He passed back in 2000 and Baby is still there caring for Jimmy."

"Jimmy's not married?"

"Oh no," Ammie scolded. "You should know better than that. Remember? He's the one that was poisoned in the war. They say he shouldn't have children, and between you, me and the wall, it's said he can't function as a husband."

I puzzled this out. "You mean Vietnam? He's not that old."

"No, after that. He was poisoned by the gas we let loose down on that island, in that little war. It was a tragic thing. He come home just white as a haunt and his hands shaking so he couldn't hold his fork to eat. Near broke my heart, it did, when I saw him at the summer social the year he got home."

"But he's better now?"

"Sure. It still poisons him, though, and he won't poison a wife and child."

"That's horrible." I felt his pain—for needing to so severely isolate himself in such a way. I did remember him, an idle bit of gossip on a summer's eve.

Ammie sighed and pulled a strawberry from the bowl. She capped it expertly and popped the entire fruit into her mouth. We sat in companionable silence a long time as she chewed thoughtfully.

I knew I had to investigate Thibideaux. War did funny things to people's minds. It could be that his enforced isolation was taking its toll and he had snapped in some subtle way. Maybe he envied the Price family's happiness. Though it was depressing to admit, I could see that Patty and Landa had built a good life together here in the Price home and had made a good home for Kissy.

"Well, it's on to dessert for me," Ammie said, rising, "though by the looks of those berries, I'm not sure but what that pie'll be all syrup." She eyed me with an accusatory glare.

I laughed and raised my hands in a defensive posture. "Hey, now, give a gal a break. I've only been here an hour or so."

Ammie laughed and snatched the basket of strawberries from the table and pressed it to her chest. She sobered and leaned forward meeting me almost nose-to-nose. "You find him, baby girl. Do that for Ammie and do it fast. Let us see his face and I'll make sure you get all the strawberries you could ever want."

The ferocious look in those deep brown eyes surprised me. "Yes, ma'am," I said.

CHAPTER SIX

The dining room at Fortune Farm was smaller than might have been expected, given the large size of the sprawling farmhouse. Carved into when a pantry was built onto the kitchen, it was nonetheless a cozy room.

Kissy was adorable. Cherubic with the innate charm all four-year-olds possess, she sat at the head of the long wooden table, contentedly dipping her fingers into a large crystal bowl of tossed salad and munching away. She was a pretty child, with long, dark curls that wisped around her face and tumbled solidly down her back. Her face was still baby round, with large brown eyes that gleamed with intelligence. This intelligence was further manifested by the way she greeted me after quietly eying me for a long while.

"Are you MomPatty's friend? The private vestigator?"

"Yes. My name is Denni. You must be Kissy."

She watched me with an eerie calm as she chewed on nibbles of radish she'd filched from the bowl. "Kissy stands for Katherine Grace. It's just a nickname."

I had to admire the erudite delivery. "So I guessed. Denni is too. It's short for Denise."

"I like Denise best."

"It's okay. People started calling me Denni when I was little like you. It just kind of stuck."

"Are you gonna take care of the bad men being mean to us? Lookit what they did." She turned her right cheek away and swept back her heavy hair. I saw a large horizontal bruise running along her jaw and into her hairline in back. There was a long raw area where hair had been ripped out by the roots.

"They really hurt you, huh?"

Kissy reached for a carrot slice. "Uh-huh. With a big stick or something. My ear still hurts."

"That must have been awful. Can you tell me what you remember?"

She sat back and screwed her mouth into a crooked bow. "I was getting those prickies…"

"Milkweed pods," interjected Ammie, entering with the soup. "She collects them and uses the down to make hair for her swamp dolls."

Ammie eyed Kissy to see if she'd been chewing. Kissy stared back with wide, innocent eyes.

"Hands off the salad," Ammie said as she disappeared into the kitchen.

"So you were out collecting pods. Were you supposed to be out there all by yourself?"

Kissy shook her head in the negative. "They were all busy and mad, so I went by myself. MomLanda said it was okay." She reached for a spinach leaf.

"Busy and mad. Why?"

She shrugged and studied my face. Her eyes rested on my dark, short hair, then my dark brown eyes and then my large mouth. "You're really pretty," she said finally. "I like how black your hair is."

"Thank you. Yours is really pretty too."

"MomLanda usually braids it but…," she sighed as if the tolerance of the world lived in her heart. "It's been very weird around here."

"I know. That's why MomPatty called me—to see if I can help make it a good place again."

"Because you're a private vestigor."

I chuckled at the mispronunciation. "Well, actually I'm an insurance investigator, but that's pretty much the same thing."

"Do you think you can do it?"

"What? Make the bad guys stop? I hope so, but first I need to find out who's doing it," I said with a sigh.

"Who's been doing what?" John Clyde asked as he entered the room.

"Uncle!" Kissy cried, tumbling off her chair in a froth of curly hair, denim, sneakers and striped shirt.

"Hey, sweetums, give us a kiss." John Clyde crouched on one knee and playfully encouraged the child's pummeling and loud, wet smooches.

I smiled, watching the two, but sobered as Patty and Yolanda entered with Human at their side. John Clyde looked up and his smile fell. I realized suddenly that Landa and John Clyde harbored a certain antagonism between them. I made a mental note to ask Patty about that as soon as we had a few moments alone.

Kissy moved to Patty's side and John Clyde and Landa squared off on opposite corners of the table. I stood and watched everyone take their usual seats before choosing mine. John Clyde sat to my right, Kissy sat at the head. Patty was across from John Clyde and Landa was next to her. Ammie was still in the kitchen, and it was not unusual to start without her.

"Kissy, would you say the blessing for us, please?" Patty asked, one hand smoothing the child's hair from her eyes.

"Yes, MomPatty," Kissy replied and lilted a hurried version of the Lord's Prayer.

Patty sighed and Landa moved to serve soup into individual bowls. Kissy reached to serve salad, but the tongs proved too large for her tiny hands so Patty moved to help.

DAY TWO

CHAPTER SEVEN

I loved summers at Fortune Farm and southwestern Louisiana. The hot sun rising in the east behind the lush greenery of cane and hay always seemed like such a new beginning, much more so than Virginia's mountain-buried mornings. The flat two hundred acres of Price farmland stretched as far as the eye could see, all the way to the Sabine River on the west and almost into Lake Charles on the east. The southernmost part bordered on Sabine Lake and from there one could nearly see into Port Arthur, Texas. Some of the land currently lay fallow while other acres burgeoned with dark green sugarcane or waving hay grass.

"All right, Patty, what's going on here?" I asked the next morning as we walked across the cleared field behind the house. We had gotten a late start, mostly because I had overslept, tired from my day of travel. I had fallen into bed, asleep, I believe, even before my head hit the pillow. The family and I had taken our time over one of Ammie's excellently prepared breakfasts to catch up on new times and reminisce about old.

Now we were still taking our time. Kissy ran ahead, leaping across the tough hillocks of grass that marked this seldom-used southern end of the property. Human ran along beside her, racing ahead and then running back as if to tease her for not keeping up. Our path converged onto a wide dirt drive lying parallel to a long, low barn-like building. Huge, serpentine tractors filled orderly bays. They'd been repaired— gas cartridges and fuel lines replaced—and rested, awaiting active duty.

"What?" Patty stopped and gazed curiously at me.

"John Clyde and Landa. What's the deal?"

"I don't know…about a year ago they started getting on one another's nerves. Then when Mama died, it seemed to get worse. I'm not sure why. I used to think he plain didn't like her, but now…maybe it's jealousy, like I spend too much time with her."

"I disagree. Look how much time y'all spend together working on this place. You and John Clyde are together every day."

"I know," Patty agreed. "But we're not working together so much. I'm not sure what his problem is. And getting someone to talk about anything around here is like pulling teeth."

"What about Landa? You trust her?"

"Sure, why wouldn't I? We've been together four years and I've never seen her do anything that aroused doubt." She paused and studied me. "She's a good gal, Denni. Even you'd like her if you got to know her."

I turned away, speechless. What could I say? I did not like Landa, and it wasn't all because Patty chose her over me. Some of it was a difference in personalities. I saw her as a blurred character. She had no definition. I like things cut and dried.

"So how did you discover the tractors had been tampered with?"

"John Clyde did. He came out with a crew of men to start cutting the hay on Crossbottom. He was pissed. Some of the tank caps had even been tossed in the high grass over there.

He was hung over from the night before so he was especially obnoxious."

I looked in the direction she pointed. "Has he been drinking a lot?"

We paused, and I walked a short way into the high weeds. A wind was blowing from the west, drying the layer of sweat that covered my brow.

"Yeah, I'm worried about that. Ammie told me about three weeks ago that our liquor bill was up. He never drank this much when Mama was alive." She sighed and her face took on a pained, frightened expression. "I'm so tired, Denni. Maybe us moving into the house here was a big mistake. It seems like so much more is asked of me now. I'm not so sure I have it in me to keep on pretending everything will be all right."

"It will," I hastened to reassure her.

"I hope so. Listen, I'll leave you to your PI stuff. We'll be over at Eastquarter if you need me."

"Eastquarter?"

Patty grinned, no doubt remembering how I never could grasp all the pet names the Prices had assigned to various segments of farmland. "Just follow the Sabine south and you'll find us."

I looked west to where the wide Sabine River traveled the edge of Price land and on toward the lake and then the mighty Gulf of Mexico.

"Ruddy Bayou—where's that?" I asked.

"South of here, where the Sabine meets the lake. Before the beaches. You want me to take you over now?"

"I thought Sabine Lake was all industrial now."

Patty nodded, but she was clearly anxious to get to work. "Most of it is. It was still pretty when I was real little. You remember they had some parks and beaches? Well, it's different now. There's several plans underway, though, to reclaim some parks, and there's still some pretty areas. Ruddy was originally too rocky and grown up for the boats to come in, but that squall we had a couple years ago cleaned out a lot of the crap.

I'm sure someone will come in and develop it once John Clyde and I pass on."

"What about Kissy? She'll get the farm unless John Clyde decides to have some kids."

"Yeah, but will I care then? Hell, she's already a lot more progressive than any of us. She'd probably sell out and move to a condo in California."

I laughed, agreeing with her. "I believe you're right about that."

Patty turned suddenly and looked to her left. I heard it then too. It was Human barking with a sharp staccato sound. Then Kissy's voice reached us. She was screaming for help.

CHAPTER EIGHT

By the time we reached Kissy, she had quieted—as if accepting her fate. She was chin deep in a sinkhole of water and dark, sandy sludge. Ribbons of murky, viscous mud framed her round, oddly calm eyes. Human raced back and forth along the edge of the sinkhole, clearly frustrated at being unable to rescue her. His whines of fear raised gooseflesh on my arms.

"Kissy! Oh baby, what happened?" Patty said as she lay on her stomach and tried to reach Kissy. Her hands fell a foot or so short.

"I dunno, MomPat. We were running and…" She lifted one hand to reach toward her mother and abruptly sank two inches.

"Damn. It's quicksand," Patty muttered.

"You're not serious," I said. I could only stare in horror as the child struggled to keep her mouth above the slimy, sandy mud. Then I started looking around for something, anything, to throw in and use to pull the girl out.

"Be still, baby," Patty called to Kissy. "Denni, hold on to my legs. I'm gonna grab her."

I threw myself on the ground and tightened my arms around both of Patty's denim-clad calves. She had on work boots, and I was grateful for that as it made a better handle against my shoulders. We inched forward, more of Patty's upper body gradually advancing above the lower level of the muck in the sinkhole.

"Whoa! Wait…" She gasped as an elbow was sucked down into the mud. She turned her body, easing the arm loose as her other arm reached toward Kissy. The child's mouth was in mud now and I could see only her panicked eyes and sand-covered nose as she struggled for air. I inched Patty forward with new urgency.

"Get her, Patty. We don't have much time," I said through gritted teeth.

"I'm trying, damnit," Patty growled. She began to sob, in frustration, I'm sure, but she never paused as she stretched herself as far over the trench as possible, looping one arm about Kissy's head, plunging her other hand under the quicksand in search of Kissy's armpit. She needed a way to lever the child out because the heavy, saturated mud was pulling against her.

"Pull me, Denni, pull hard. This won't be easy," she gasped.

I looked up one more time and saw her trying to blow wet sand from Kissy's nostrils as she lifted her slightly.

I dug in the toes of my sneakers and, using my hips and elbows, edged away from the muddy sinkhole. I wrapped my arms more tightly around Patty's legs and pulled as hard as I could. It seemed as though hours passed, but I was eventually able to roll myself into a sitting position and pull both of them to safety, digging in my heels and using my full body weight and my arm strength. We rolled apart, and I fell back, my arms quivering from the exertion.

Kissy, clearly frightened by the experience, cuddled into Patty's lap and popped one dirty, sand-caked thumb into her mouth. She stared at me with wide, blank eyes. Patty had her own eyes closed and was holding her daughter tightly, rocking to and fro and uttering soothing sounds. I watched them, my heart slowly returning to a normal rhythm.

Studying the sinkhole, I was perplexed. I didn't remember anything like this from years ago when Patty and I had stolen kisses while walking the grounds of Fortune. The hole was huge, about eight feet in diameter. The rippled sand and wet black dirt center was about eighteen inches lower than the surrounding, firmer soil. "What is this thing, Patty?" I gasped, taking deep breaths to calm myself. "Have you always had drop-offs like this?"

"No." She stopped rocking, but her hands still worked to clean and calm the eerily silent child in her lap. "It's normal this close to sea level, though. I think it was that storm we had. It cleared out a lot of protective stuff that kept the land solid. I bet the water's been seeping in since and undermining the land."

"Does John Clyde know about this?"

She shook her head, anger replacing the paralyzing fear she'd probably felt before. "No, how could he? I told you this has never happened before."

"You need to do a sound survey. This is dangerous as hell."

Patty ignored my pedantic rambling and started rocking again.

I stood. "Let's get y'all home."

Patty sighed and tried to rise. Kissy cried out and clung to Patty, momentarily knocking her off balance. I reached to steady them and held them both close for a good long time.

CHAPTER NINE

Back at the house Landa and Ammie shrieked with horror when they saw our muddy, sandy burden. Kissy went to Landa as if numb, her now clean thumb irresistibly finding her mouth again. She hadn't spoken during the entire walk home, even when Patty and I had taken turns carrying her, and this worried me. I felt helpless, though, unable to do anything but stand by like a cement post as the other women rushed her upstairs and into a warm bath. I followed meekly, and when everything seemed under control, I left the busy women and made my way outside again.

The Louisiana afternoon had strolled in with an easy swagger, and I took a deep breath of the humid air. The cloying scent of warm, wet grass was a familiar, long-lost friend. Trying to be useful and determined to continue searching for clues, I went toward the goat pen. Two of the baby goats had survived and they watched my approach with cautious eyes. After mulling over whether to trust this stranger, they came to me after I'd stood by the fence quietly for a few minutes. Their little brown noses were soft with new fur, and I found comfort in their begging stance and their curious licks of my fingers.

"I wish you could talk," I told them with a sigh.

Leaving the goats, I moved away along the road that led south to the Sabine River. It was a good fifteen-minute walk and I churned it, walking now more for exercise and for stress relief after the morning's excitement. Fortune Farm was actually a small farm, only about two hundred acres. Most was cultivated hay or cane land, but this land to the south was swampy and its blackish soil was heavy with shale. I had forgotten about the brutality of the Louisiana slanting sun and humidity and was glad I had chosen shorts and good walking shoes to wear that morning. My only regret was that I didn't have a hat and sunglasses. The dirt and gravel road seemed to stretch on forever.

Movement farther along, by the side of the road, caught my attention. I spied the farmhand, Alejandro, standing beside one of the yellow, insectile farm tractors. He was acting oddly, looking over his shoulder toward the Price home as if afraid of being seen. This piqued my interest, of course, so I moved slowly left until I was shielded by a small grove of roadside underbrush. It took several minutes to understand what he was doing, but I finally realized he was wrapping some type of oblong, thick object in burlap. He was using baling twine from a large spindle on the back of the tractor and twisting it securely around the wrapped bundle. Every now and then he would look toward the big white farmhouse then busily resume his task. He didn't see me watching.

When he was almost finished, I stirred and made my way over toward him. He heard my approach and resembled a deer caught in car headlights.

"Your name is Alexander, right?"

"Alejandro, miss," he replied in heavily accented English. "Alejandro Cezanne."

"I'm sorry. Alejandro. My name is Denni Hope. I'm an investigator, a friend of Patty's, and I'm looking into the events that have been happening here at the Prices's place. Have you seen anything suspicious? Strange people, things in odd places? Anything like that?"

I watched his face closely, looking for one of the myriad ways an astute person can tell that another is lying. He was a handsome man, with short, dark hair that swept back from his deeply tanned forehead. His face was lean, with cheeks high and aquiline. In stature, he was about my height, five foot seven, but more muscular. He rippled with lean muscle under his close fitting T-shirt and jeans.

He shook his head in the negative, mouth in a grim line and eyes unreadable. "No, nothing like this. I work spreading the fertilizer, the water. I'm in the fields."

I eyed the bundle he held casually in one hand. "You're not in the fields today."

His eyes rolled once, nervously. Aha, gotcha, I thought to myself.

"No, I came to get the tractor to haul some fill bags back to the shed for Carlos. He sent me here."

"But you're not up in the tractor." I allowed my eyes to linger on the bundle. "And what's this you have here?"

He didn't look at the bundle. Instead his eyes sought mine. "I don' want no trouble, miss. Please, I've done nothing wrong."

"Now, Alejandro." I kept my voice very calm while my body fell into fight-or-flight mode. If this was the man responsible for the mayhem and he felt cornered...well, anything could happen. "What do you mean? I haven't said you've done anything wrong."

He hesitantly extended the bundle. "It was on the road here. In the weeds. I found it there."

"What is it?" I took it from him gingerly. Was this something related to my investigation?

He shrugged. "I didn't want the misses to be upset seeing it. I was gonna hide it away. In one of the barns."

I untwisted the twine and peeled back the burlap. Resting in my hands was a two-by-two board about two feet long. It had some age on it and one end was jagged, with a partially sawn edge, as if someone had tried to saw through it with a power tool and the board had broken prematurely. The other end was mill-sawn, stained green, and had the faded words Intercoastal Woodworks branded into it. Several strands of long, dark hair and a dark substance like clotted blood was entwined in the shredded end.

I studied Alejandro. "You found this? Where exactly? Can you show me?"

He looked surprised. "Yes, of course. I think it was what hurt the little miss. I was afraid…" He shrugged again.

I wasn't exactly buying his Mr. Innocent routine, but a man *is* innocent until proven guilty. I'd give him the benefit of doubt. He led me just off the road and pointed to where he'd found the board. Up high on the tractor seat, he had spied the blondness of the board amongst the pale greenery alongside the road.

"Alejandro, can you take me to where Kissy was hit? Is it far?"

"Not very, but we should go down on the tractor. The walk is long, and it might grow dark before you come back."

I held on to the burlap-wrapped board and followed him to the tractor, where he checked the straps on a low trailer behind it that was piled high with bags of fertilizer. Obviously, Alejandro had been returning these unused ones to the storage shed so they wouldn't be out in the damp all night. I had been at the farm long enough to know that the bags would be used to fill a small spreader that was used in the lesser fields closest to the river. The larger tractors in the bigger fields would attach to huge vats of commercial fertilizer.

I perched behind Alejandro on the running board and we lurched into motion. I had the good sense to berate myself mentally for venturing into the bayou with a man I barely knew, one who could be responsible for hurting Patty's family and business. I tried to think positive thoughts as we moved farther from the big white farmhouse and safety. I was somewhat comforted by the small but heavy pistol strapped into the underarm holster beneath my over shirt but was relieved, nevertheless, when Alejandro paused the tractor on a grassy bank below a field full of busy laborers. He switched off the engine and pointed toward the river. "Go right and go fifty yards until the river changes. I found more boards there when I was washing seeds off my shirt."

"And that's Ruddy Bayou?"

He nodded and drew a bandana from his back pocket to swipe across the back of his neck. "They say the little miss was found walking here, with blood on her face." He squinted at me. "I'm telling you, miss. I didn't have nothin' to do with that. I just work in the fields."

"Thanks, Alejandro. I appreciate your help. This is evidence, though, and if you find anything else, you have to bring it to me immediately, okay?"

I took the board with me, not wanting it to disappear suddenly. I think I was also hoping possibly to match it to something there at the site.

Alejandro nodded. "I will unload the trailer and come back for you."

I waved to show I heard. The stirred-up mosquitoes were loving me as I trudged through high grass. I knew I'd be seeking out more of Ammie's healing balm when I returned to the farmhouse.

I reached the edge of the Sabine River after walking about ten feet. The water, sluggish and muddy, rolled by slowly as it made its way to the lake. Bald cyprus islands prevented me from seeing the other side here, and the water looked dark and mysterious. I had a sudden insight into how scary it must have been for Kissy fighting her way back to its surface. The thought of this angered me, and I began to search the area with keen intensity.

Methodically, I mentally divided a twenty-foot area of riverbank into foot-sized grids. I walked slowly through each one, my eyes examining every blade of grass. At one point, where the bank sloped down from the road, I discovered large patches where the grass had been plowed under the mud by what appeared to be wide truck tires. I knelt and examined them more closely. A few small board sections, similar to the one I held in my hand, were scattered about the bank. Some floated in the shallow, marshy water.

Standing back, I studied the scene a few minutes and surmised that the truck had been escaping up the bank toward the road with, no doubt, an open truck bed, and the pieces of wood had fallen out. I thought about who might be foolish enough to drive a truck along the bayou, a risky business because the land was not secure in the least and a heavy vehicle could disappear in a heartbeat. The weight of a large truck like that was usually kept a good twenty yards from the water and certainly not on a sloping, slippery bank.

I walked on, along the gentle slant of the bayou, pausing when I found a tousled pile of milkweed pods. I touched them sadly. Studying the immediate surroundings, I could see how it might have happened. He had waited there, behind a small grove of cyprus, his truck parked perilously low to hide it from the road. Maybe he'd been watching the family's routines for some time, hoping to find Kissy alone. Had he followed her from the house, predicting her path? Did he mean to kill her? Or just terrify the family? Had Kissy surprised him somehow? She hadn't said anything to that effect, only that she had been hit from behind. What kind of cruel monster would whale on a small child with a board?

Unable to find definitive answers no matter how tightly I scrunched my brow, I finally gave up and oriented myself for the walk back to the road to wait for Alejandro. I pulled the burlap more snugly around the board I carried, knowing I would have to give it to the police chief in Brethren. I would also tell him about the boards that had spilled from the truck. If they could be matched to this one, then later to some in the perpetrator's vehicle, this nightmare would be over.

CHAPTER TEN

They were sprawled on the bed in Kissy's cozy little bedroom, the two of them, their dark heads bent together over a book with large, colorful photographs. I moved closer and realized it was an encyclopedia. Patty pointed to a small reptile and Kissy grunted.

"Fire-bellied newt, MomPat. You thought I forgot it, didn't you?"

Patty smiled at her daughter, but her face twisted with concern when she caught sight of me. She stood.

"Hey there, how are you? Ammie said you were walking the land."

"Looking for clues, anything," I said as I dropped into one of the chairs at Kissy's little decorated table. I lifted a Barbie doll and started dressing it with some of the doll clothing that was scattered about.

"Any luck?"

"This is a fire-bellied newt, Denni. Wanna see?" Kissy turned the book so the black and red newt was visible. I stood and walked over so I could see it. It really was beautiful.

"That's so cool," I said, studying the photograph. I turned and studied Kissy.

"Are you all right?" I asked.

Kissy didn't answer, and I could tell that the close call of the morning was something she just plain did not want to talk about. Instead her interest in the book grew even more keen as she disregarded my question.

Patty, the diligent mother, tucked a strand of hair behind Kissy's ear. "We're doing okay, Miss Denni," she said in a breathy voice. "We're going to be just fine."

"Patty, we need to talk," I said. "You got a minute?"

"Sure. What's up?" Patty placed the toys she'd been retrieving from the floor onto the shelves in one corner of Kissy's ultrafeminine pink and lavender bedroom. "I guess this was a pretty sucky first day of vacation for you, wasn't it?" she added.

"It's okay. Just glad everything turned out all right. Let's sit over here." I guided Patty to the table and pulled out one of the tiny chairs for her.

"Have you noticed anything unusual about John Clyde lately?" I asked as soon as we were seated.

"You mean other than worrying his ulcer into acting up? No, nothing really. Just the drinking." She watched me closely. I averted my gaze. I couldn't explain to her why my spidey-sense was acting up concerning her brother. I couldn't explain it to myself.

"Think hard, hon. This could be important. Anything different since your mama died?"

"Well, there was one instance that pops into my mind. The week after Mama passed was horrible and John Clyde used to go into her room and just kind of sit there. I couldn't bear to do that because it just hurt me too much."

"But he would? Just sit there? For how long?"

Patty nodded and continued, "Hours, like when it was raining. One day I went to call him for supper and he was crying. Sitting in Mama's wicker rocker and crying. Just tore my heart up."

"That seems pretty natural, Patty. You know you did your share of crying too."

"Right. But what was strange was that when I went to hug him, he hid something, slid it under his leg so I wouldn't see," she explained.

"What was it? Could you tell?"

"No, and it's been working on my mind ever since, like an otter after a crawdad." She sat back and sighed.

"And you have no idea what it could have been?" I asked.

"Nope. And it's so unlike John Clyde to hide anything from me. We're so close…were so close. I just couldn't ask him about it, not then when he was so sad."

"Strange." I rubbed my eyes with both hands and leaned forward to rest my elbows on my knees.

"Yes, it is. And I don't even know if it's important. With all this insanity that's been going on, he's just not been himself at all."

"How do you mean? Can you be more specific?"

"It's hard to pin down, Denni. He's been distracted, angry."

"Angry?" I looked over at her. "Like at Yolanda."

"Well, yeah, and he's angry Mama died, like the rest of us. Mine's gone away some, finally. I'm not so sure his has."

"How do you mean?"

Patty drew fingers through her dark hair. "You are so aggravating! I can't explain it. Why do you ask so many blasted questions?"

I eyed Patty with disbelief, and we began laughing together. Years rolled away, and it was like it used to be. Like we were still together. I sighed.

"I know, that's your job," Patty chortled.

"And just what do you mean by that?" I countered and the comment set us laughing again.

Patty sobered first and I could see the pain in her face.

"It'll be okay, Patty," I said, wanting very badly to reach for her hand but realizing it would be a bad move for both of us at this moment. "No one will hurt Kissy—or any of you, for that matter. Not while I'm here."

"I know. But just for my own peace of mind, I've emailed Erica and asked her to come get Kissy. They have such a good time together and Kissy needs that right now. And I need to know she's safely removed from whatever is going on here," Patty said.

"Erica?"

"You remember. Mom's best friend—since they were little girls. A real sweetheart. You've met her."

"Is that the one Megs had all those pictures of?"

Patty's face brightened. "Right! That's her. Mama was just crazy about her. She lives over in Jackson with her husband, Clayton."

"Does Kissy know she's going over there? Is she okay about it?"

"Lord, yes, she adores Erica. You might not mention it to John Clyde, though."

"John Clyde? Why?"

"He's been a little strange about her too since Mama died. I have no idea what that's all about."

I screwed my face into a mask of confusion. "Did he like her before?"

Patty thought a minute, bending over, fingers picking at loose threads in the soft center rug. "Well, he could always take her or leave her, you know how teenaged boys are. Erica's the sweetest, most inoffensive person we know, though. It's just totally irrational that he's bad-mouthing her all of a sudden."

I nodded. "Very. John Clyde doesn't bad-mouth much of anybody, usually."

Patty sighed. "I guess Mama's death just did a number on all of us. Thank goodness me and John Clyde aren't arguing over the business like other families do. I couldn't bear that, not after losing Mama."

"I never would have imagined you would. You've always been able to work stuff out," I said reassuringly.

Kissy had wandered over, and now she inserted herself into the circle of Patty's arms. Her thumb found her mouth again as she pressed back into her mother. I reached over and patted her protruding stomach. "Where's your MomLanda?" I asked her.

Her thumb slid from her mouth for a quick moment. "Ice cream cake." The thumb slotted back in.

I lifted a questioning eyebrow to Patty. "Ice cream cake?"

Patty laughed. "For a bedtime snack. To make Little Bit here feel better."

"Ahhh," I said, nodding. "Sounds like one heck of a great idea. Can I have some too?"

Kissy nodded and smiled at me. She really was an adorable child.

"Hey, Patty, when are you going into Brethren next?"

"Tomorrow, why? I have a meeting with the bank board and planned to pick up a few household things. Do you need a ride in?"

"Yes, that would be great. I can do what I need to do, then hang out til you're done, if that's okay with you."

"Can I go, Mommy?" Kissy asked sweetly. Patty grimaced at her.

"I'm sorry, babykins. MomLanda is off and she wanted to do some stuff with you."

Kissy nodded and, sweeping up one of the Barbie dolls from the table, she flopped onto a pile of floor cushions and started cooing to the doll.

I smiled at Patty. "She's easy."

"Ha!" she barked. "You don't know her very well."

We laughed and went downstairs together to see if Landa had returned.

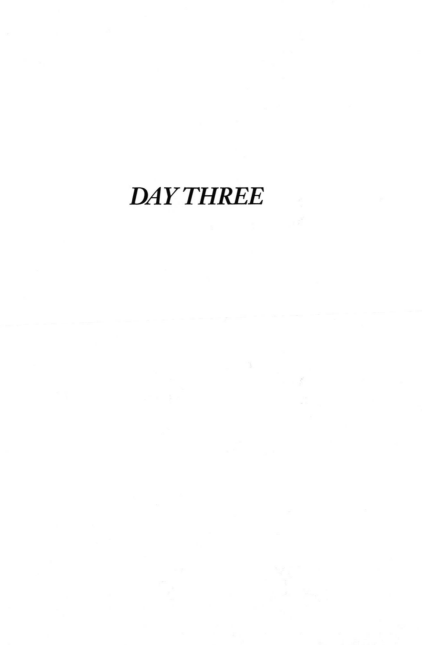

DAY THREE

CHAPTER ELEVEN

A warm rain was falling when we arrived in downtown Brethren the next morning. Not that there was a downtown in Brethren *per se*; it was more like a main street with a string of faded shops and a square of flag-flying government buildings. The survivors that had outlasted the storms. It was all much the same as when I'd left, filled with tall, weathered, wood-sided buildings no doubt listed on a historical register somewhere. Even the retired or disabled old men who wallpapered the front benches of the storefronts appeared the same.

"So you'll be okay?" Patty asked as she pulled her blue Taurus close to the curb in front of the drug store.

"Yep, just going over to Little John's to see the mausoleum, then get a feel for what's going on here in town," I said.

I hadn't told her about the length of wood Alejandro had found. I needed more information before broaching that subject. I had it with me, though, barely squeezing it into my backpack, because I planned to drop it off with the Brethren Police Department.

"So are you sure five's not too late to pick you up?"

"You know me." I grinned at her. "I'll start running my mouth and will probably be late meeting you. Enjoy your day."

I shut the door, and Patty, with a short wave of acknowledgment, moved into the light Main Street traffic.

I stood and looked along the major artery of Main Street, which branched off Highway 82. It was lined with even more ancient businesses that had received grant monies at some point to polish themselves up, as if to prove that the economy of Brethren really was thriving.

Patty had dropped me off on the sidewalk in front of the Rexall Drug Store, now run by Heywood Lyon. At least it had been four years ago. I studied the faded window offerings for a moment but decided not to go inside. Daylight was burning and I really did need to get to the bottom of some things. I only had a week to solve this mystery, and I'd be damned if I was gonna slink away without knowing—and dealing with—the full truth.

Main Street stretched west to Sabine Lake, where I could see the dusky blue waters and the skeletal outlines of the dock cranes, and then east to hook up with the Sabine National Wildlife Refuge, which was mainly bayou country. Patty had told me on the drive in that the wildlife refuge, where we had often hiked and picnicked, had been forever changed by the storm of 2008. Parts of it had even been closed for more than a year, undergoing repair work.

I thought back to the years I'd spent in Louisiana. I chuckled as I remembered the time we'd been driving my Jeep over to the NWR and had encountered an eight-foot alligator sunning himself in the middle of a wide back road. We had laughed and picnicked on the tailgate of the Jeep, waiting patiently for animal control to come out and move the big lug off the tarmac. That had been a fun, if frightening, day. I had been fascinated by the huge, bump-covered creature with its two-inch-long yellow teeth. It had been my first encounter with one but would not be my last.

I pushed memory aside and moved east along Main Street. The Brethren City Police Force office was a small building that fronted on Cleveland Street, one of Highway 82's many side streets. Inside, the air smelled of unwashed underarms and cigarette smoke. A very large woman of color was manning the front desk, her gaze fixed on a computer screen. I stepped up to the desk.

"Excuse me." I swung my backpack off my shoulder and rested it on the pocked wooden floor.

The receptionist turned to me, her dark eyes curious, the brown irises resting in yellowed sclera. Then she smiled and I felt myself responding to her gap-toothed grin with a smile of my own.

"Hey, sugah, what can I do for you?" she asked, her voice a deep and pleasant alto.

"Hello, my name is Denni Hope, from Virginia. I'm here staying with my friends over at the Price farm outside town and was wondering if I could talk to…" I checked my notebook for the name Ammie had given me. "Captain Armbruster Seychelles. It shouldn't take long."

The receptionist leaned forward and clasped two sausage-fingered hands on the desktop. The fingers bore several heavy gold rings and were topped with inch-long, bright red fingernails. "He's in the back, hon. You want me to go fetch him for you?"

"Oh no, I can find him. What's he look like?"

"Well, I think Buster's just the most beautiful man you've ever seen," she exclaimed avidly. "He's real tall, black but with big old green eyes from his mama's side of the family. You can't miss him. Just go on back and take the last left."

"Good looking, huh?" I said chuckling.

"Oh, sister, I'm telling you the truth…" She burst into peals of low laughter.

I waved at her, lifted my backpack and headed back. I was bemoaning the BPD's lack of security. I sure hoped the police in this bucolic little town got their act together before they welcomed a killer with an automatic assault weapon in a backpack instead of a blood-stained board.

I passed through a mostly deserted room with a handful of desks in it, then into a narrow hallway lined by open and closed office doors. The end of the hallway appeared to be a lunchroom, judging by the long table and chairs and other kitchen-like elements.

I paused outside the last door on the left. Sure enough, Captain Armbruster Seychelles was handsome. His long legs were resting on his desk as he leaned back in his office chair reading a paperback novel. He was wearing the dark blue BPD uniform, short sleeved, and several bars and pins decorated the collars and front panel. I tapped gently on the doorjamb, and he turned those magnificent green eyes on me. They were mesmerizing, especially when taken as part of his dark, African American features.

He lowered his legs and sat up as I quickly introduced myself and explained that I was helping Patty and John Clyde find out who was behind the harmful incidents at Fortune Farm.

"Yes, ma'am," he said, his voice deep and slow. "I've been working on that case, but we're having the devil's own time finding out anything. Seems like this perpetrator is a ghost, he's in and out of there so fast."

"Well, I hope you won't feel as though I'm stepping on toes. I just want to help out my friends and who knows, maybe I'll get lucky."

"Yes, ma'am," he agreed. "I guess you want to see the filed reports?"

"If you wouldn't mind." I pulled my backpack up and rested it on the chair in front of his desk. "I happened upon one of the farmhands by the name of Alejandro the other day. He was wrapping something in burlap, sorta down by the Sabine. When I called him on it, he showed me this."

I placed the burlap-wrapped board on the desk before him. Impressing me, he opened a side drawer and took out vinyl gloves and slipped them on before unwrapping the bundle.

"It's a board," he said, glancing at me. He looked more closely at the end. "Ah, I see. This must be the one that hit the child over the head."

"Yes, sir, that's what I thought as well."

He fixed discerning eyes upon me, and I suddenly realized I'd hate to be the bad guy apprehended by this man. "So why was this Alejandro trying to hide it? Do you think he's involved?"

"I did at first," I answered, removing my backpack and claiming the seat. "I'm suspicious by nature anyway."

He chuckled and pulled the wrapping more tightly around the board, as if to protect it.

"But after I spoke with him a while, I've come to believe him when he said he was trying to spare Patty and Yolanda from having to see it. The board appears to have been thrown out right on the side of the road after the perpetrator hit Kissy with it."

"So, gut level, you believe he wasn't the one." It was a statement that begged for corroboration.

"Yes, sir. He also took me to where Kissy said she'd been hit, and there were more boards there with similar markings. It's my opinion that the perpetrator drove a truck along Ruddy Bayou and waited for the child to come along. He then used wood that he had on the back of his truck, and when he went to drive off, he got stuck on an incline and dropped a portion of the load off the back of his truck. You can see the skid marks of his tires and also the pile of rough cut lumber."

"Lucky he got out at all," Seychelles said. "He must not be from around here because anyone from the bayou knows how foolish it is to drive a heavy vehicle close to the water."

He sat back and laced his long brown fingers across his abdomen. "You know, two patrolmen searched that area where she said she was hit."

I shrugged and frowned. "It was early in the game. Your men may not have put two and two together without the board Alejandro found. It was in the weeds beside the road, sorta up near the house."

He nodded and sighed. "That's true. But maybe I'll mosey over and snoop around now."

"I always say two heads are better than one," I told him, grinning. "Look on the east bank where the lake meets Ruddy, just where that big clump of cyprus knees hides the other side."

"Thank you. I'll do that. So, you do insurance investigation." His eyes lit with interest. "What's that like?"

"Boring for the most part," I replied truthfully. "Lots of following people around and slogging through Internet sites. You wouldn't believe the things so-called 'injured' people post on their Facebook sites."

Seychelles laughed heartily. "Oh, I can imagine."

I stood, needing to get to the mausoleum. "I'll leave that with you?"

"Yes, ma'am," he said, nodding and rising to his feet. He was imposing, a couple inches taller than six feet. He dug around on his desk and found a business card. He scribbled on the front of it. "Here's my cell. Don't hesitate to call me if you need anything from us or find out anything else."

I took the card and pocketed it. "Sure, thank you. Will you please let me know what you find out from the forensics on the board? And when I can drop by and pick up the copies of those case files?"

I pulled out one of my business cards from my wallet and handed it to him. "My cell's at the bottom and you can also call Fortune Farm. I'll be staying there until Saturday."

He stood thoughtfully. "You mean you're gonna try to find out who did this in just a week's time?"

I smiled ruefully. "Yes, sir. I never did say I was smart now, did I?"

We laughed and he ushered me into the front room. Several uniformed officers had returned to their desks and they watched us curiously as we passed.

"I see you found him," the receptionist said, spying us. She was standing at a filing cabinet, her heavy body attractively encased in a long, dark blue skirt and a loose red blouse.

"I did and everything you said was true," I said, lifting my eyebrows suggestively.

She snickered but composed herself when Seychelles spoke to her. "Cleo, I need you to get Dr. Flores and his team on the horn. Tell him I've got some new evidence on the Price case. Find that folder for me too, will you? And make copies of everything for Miss Hope here, while you're at it."

Cleo watched him with dreamy eyes, and I could just imagine all the carnal frolicking that was going on in her imagination. "Yes, sir. I will see to that right away, sir."

I handed her another of my cards. "You can give me a call when you get them copied. Better yet, if they're electronic you can email them to me."

Seychelles shook my hand one more time and told me goodbye before disappearing toward the back.

Cleo sighed as we watched him walk away. I nudged her playfully and she blushed. "The going away is just as good as the coming toward, isn't it?" she muttered conspiratorially.

I laughed, shook my head and slung my much lighter pack over one shoulder. "Cleo, I swear. You are something else, girl."

I stepped out into the Louisiana heat as her laughter followed behind.

CHAPTER TWELVE

Studying the map I'd called up on my cell phone, I plotted out a path to the Holding Arms Cemetery, which was called Little John's by all the locals. The tram, the Brethren version of a streetcar, stopped on Main just past the Denny's Restaurant. I hopped aboard, dropped my coins into the slot, and settled in across from a trio of gum-cracking teens, girls, who watched me suspiciously. I tried to smile at them but any friendliness they could have had toward me was well hidden under a cloak of indifference.

Brethren was laid out much like the cities of Baton Rouge or New Orleans, with beautiful courtyards hidden behind wrought iron or mud-block walls. I started out on Main, but this car's path veered into crowded subdivisions separated by small, scenic parks. They were new and refreshing oases of green amid the clutter of old buildings.

I thoroughly enjoyed the ride and was surprised, and almost disappointed, to see the stop for Iberia Commons so soon. I left the tram, with one more knowing glance back at fragile youth. I knew they would find something odd enough about me so that they could talk about it in furtive whispers once I was out of earshot. It was the way of youth, huddling together in a common mind of mockery, for safety's sake and to better homogenize.

I started walking north, glancing often at the phone clutched in my hand. Little John's looked to be only about two blocks north of the commons, but it sure felt farther. Soon the low, plaintive bleat of trumpets assailed my ears and I knew I was close.

Funerals in Louisiana are an entity unto themselves. They become, even while honoring death, a kind of living creature. There is the mournful music that precedes a grieving line of humanity, then the lift of sprightly jazz at the end of the funeral procession that assures the listener that it is okay to carry on. That though someone is gone and the void left is sad, life, light and laughter will soon come to fill that void. For that reason I loved the southern Louisiana language of death. I thought about my own mortality then and realized suddenly that this is where I wanted to have my funeral. In the Deep South, where those who came to mourn my passing would find new joy to carry on after I was gone.

I walked away from the noisy funeral parade and to the right, where I could see the heavy marble columns and gleaming face of the mausoleum at the back of the cemetery proper. I walked past the raised concrete burial plots, so common in bayou country, taking note of the fascinating names as I meandered by: Roach, Thibideaux, Breaux, Chauvin, Boudreaux, Guillio, Foret and Molaison. The raised crypt of someone named Zeophile Babineaux brought me to a complete stop. I tried to say it to myself a few times. I could not even imagine trying to teach a child to spell that on the first few days of kindergarten.

The huge mausoleum, twelve feet tall and covering at least two city blocks, was just across a white winding sidewalk from the raised burial plots. I came close to one marble-walled side, inset with thirty-two, four-stacks of crypts, two-foot-square iron plates covering each crypt, and pressed my palm to the stone's coolness. Amazing how marble never really got that warm, no matter what the ambient temperature.

I followed the scattered trail of antiseptic hothouse and silk flowers until I came to the first massive corner. I knew the Price section of this mausoleum faced east—I had been there before when Dodson Price was laid to rest. The Price crypts were in the second set of four vertical rows of crypts or the second set of eight vaults. Only four of the vaults had been used, the four on the left of the Price section. At the top was Guillaume Price, Dodson's father, and then Marigne, his mother. Third down was Dodson himself and below him rested Megs. Four more doors had yet to be inscribed, their chambers empty. I knew who they were for and the thought of Patty dying rattled me and left me motionless for a good minute. I even imagined I saw her name on one of the iron plates. I shook my head hard to clear it.

I looked left and saw immediately what Patty had been talking about. Faint outlines of the slur words could still be seen, although it was obvious there had been an effort to scrub them away. I knelt on the white wrought-iron bench that rested just below the final two horizontal vaults and closely studied the writing for some time.

Someone had left a huge white plastic basket of hothouse flowers beneath the Price section, next to the bench, and their scent wafted up to me as I perused the graffiti. I heard the ever-present hum of honeybees and took a few seconds to hope I wouldn't get stung. I absently swatted a persistent bee away.

Living near DC as I did, I knew graffiti well, and I also easily recognized a lot of gang and even personal tagging. This had nothing to do with any of that. These words—LIAR and, down lower, BITCH—had been written by one person using a Sharpie marker. The words, what I could see of them, were written sloppily and, most certainly, had been fueled by powerful emotion. I could tell this by the way the words slanted downward and by how the letters were hastily, angrily formed. The scribbled words told me a lot. First, the writing was by someone who knew Megs, or at least the Price family, well.

It seemed intimate by the way it was written—LIAR boldly across the face, then BITCH as an afterthought. Secondly, the use of the slurs implied anger and feelings of betrayal. And maybe regret. Could Megs have been involved with someone at the time of her death? Funny, the idea of Megs with someone other than Dodson had never even occurred to me.

Some investigator you are, I mentally chided myself.

Turning, I seated myself on the bench, the side away from the flowers and the bees, and, resting elbows on my knees, thought about all the troubling occurrences at Fortune Farm. Looked at from an outside perspective, they all—sugaring the tractors, Megs's personal items disappearing, even the attack on Kissy, though extreme—could very much be caused by rancor. And the markings here now led me to believe Megs was somehow directly involved.

I sighed and shifted my weight to one side, lifting my bent leg, my thigh now resting on the bench as I faced sideways. I was laying out a course of action. And a course of thought. If I turned the situation around, assuming that the events plaguing the Prices were not directed at the family so much, but more at Megs, it gave me lots of food for thought. What secrets was Megs hiding? Maybe getting to the bottom of that would allow me to understand what was happening at the farm.

My stomach grumbled loudly, and I realized I'd been woolgathering for quite some time. Sunlight was leaning heavily along the checkerboard of above ground crypts laid out before me. I rested the side of my forehead against the flat, cool marble between the Price crypts.

So, Megs, I mused silently, can you shed a little light on this, please? Your kids need to know the truth so they can get on.

I realized suddenly that the funeral music had stopped and had been silent for some time. I was surrounded by the drone of the bees and an occasional bird call. Nothing else. No doubt the funeral was over, and yet one more Brethren resident had bought a new home in this peaceful place.

I stood and laid a palm against the iron door engraved with Megs's full name and the dates of her birth and death. "I'm sorry I wasn't here to say goodbye," I said aloud. "I will miss you."

A cool breeze stirred the flowers below me and cooled my brow. It was like a caress.

I meandered slowly back the way I'd come. I wasn't thinking about the problem I was here to solve but rather musing philosophically about life and death and how it can mean so many different things to so many people. Heaven, hell or a great void? Who knew for sure?

CHAPTER THIRTEEN

Roy Ketchum's was crowded—unusual for this early on a weekday. After about five minutes of eavesdropping, however, I realized why. A cooling cylinder at the local ConAgra frozen food plant had gone down, and the first shift had been let out early.

Sipping hot, rich, chicory coffee, I studied the menu, eventually choosing an old favorite—the gumbo. Roy Ketchum's had some of the finest I'd ever had. A familiar-looking but tired waitress took my order, studying me with curiosity. I'm sure she recognized me too, yet couldn't quite place me. Four years is a long time. Giving up on the quest, she deposited some more coffee into my cup. I reached for sugar while my mind whirled with possibilities. I had less than a week to go of my vacation time so I needed to put on the old thinking cap in earnest.

I had the incidents—John Clyde hiding something, someone sugaring gas tanks, the poisoning of the goats and the attack on Kissy. What clues did I have? A board and some tire tracks. Nasty notes written on a crypt. Not very promising.

"You're losing it, Denni gal," I muttered to myself. Twelve weeks of fraud investigation school just wasn't coming through for me. Neither was the copious studying I did each month about new and ever-growing fraud possibilities. The main lesson I'd learned was to gather information. If you gathered enough information the facts would start linking themselves together and would wait for you to see them. I knew this. Obviously, I was still at the gathering information stage, because no links had shown themselves, that's for sure.

The second step was to help that process along by sorting and analyzing the information and then drawing lead-up conclusions from that info. The conclusions were then balanced against the motive list—usually money in the insurance industry—then the motives used to zero in on the perpetrator. *Voila*, fraud solved. This, though, was a tough one. I had come to believe that the one person who knew what could be causing the havoc was already dead.

I tried going back to my original thinking. Who would most gain from discrediting John Clyde and Patty? It simply had to be a competitor who wanted them out of business. Unless revenge was indeed involved. Then it could be an old enemy—or, if it was concerning Megs, perhaps a scorned lover. I knew that often those closest to someone will turn on them the quickest.

The waitress broke into my reverie by sliding a bowl of steaming gumbo across the table. It landed in front of me as if choreographed. I inhaled the incredible earthy fragrance of true Louisiana gumbo and dug in. Halfway through the bowl a familiar shock of short white blond hair off toward the front of the restaurant snared my attention. Yolanda. She was barely visible behind the high side of my booth, but I could see she was talking to someone animatedly—more animated actually than I'd ever seen her.

Chewing slowly, I leaned to my left and saw that Landa was talking to a really gorgeous woman.

Tall and almost too thin—I'm talking sixties' Twiggy thin—the woman was leaning forward, listening intently to what Landa was saying. Every now and then she would nod her head, an act that caused her long hair to move across her bare shoulders like satin sheets sweeping across a mattress. Landa was expounding grandly as if instructing the woman about something.

I took my time studying the sleekly defined woman, which turned out to be a thoroughly pleasant experience. She was dressed in low-slung, hip-hugger jeans with a wide dark belt bordering the top and had a dark purple muscle shirt tucked into the jeans. A tattered denim jacket dangled from one hand. It took me several minutes to determine what was unusual about her hair. Then it hit me. The hair was dyed to be two-toned—a long layer of jet black underneath with a somewhat shorter layer of white blond on top. The effect was startling and certainly warranted a second irresistible look.

The two women turned and I ducked back into my booth and took another bite of my cooling gumbo. Who was she? And what was she doing here with Landa? Especially when we all assumed Landa was working at her job as a health coordinator over at Ernest Glass Hospital. No, wait, it was her day off, but she was supposed to be spending it with Kissy.

I peeped carefully around the back of the booth again. They were at the counter and Landa was buying two sodas to go. They were laughing and seemed really at ease with one another. My heart lurched in pain and anger, because I knew that if Landa *was* cheating on Patty, Patty would soon be going through the same heartache I'd felt when she'd met Landa and chosen her over me. I suddenly didn't know how to feel or whether I should poke my nose into it and reveal what I'd seen.

Another thought caused my stomach to roil and the gumbo to press hard against my insides. Suppose it was Yolanda who was causing all the problems at Fortune Farm? And this was an accomplice?

CHAPTER FOURTEEN

"Oh, my stars. It *is* you. I told Emma—you know my friend Emma, Dr. Rigger's secretary? Well, I told her it had to be Denni Hope practically back from the grave. Where you been, my se-weet little galfriend?"

I recognized the voice and nonstop patter right away and was thrilled when the heavily fragranced figure swept into the seat opposite me. I took her delicate hands in mine in an awkward embrace. The scent of lily-of-the-valley lotion mixed incongruously with Estée Lauder perfume washed across me, a welcoming trigger of memory.

"Solange, you old dear, how have you been? I'm glad to see you're not at the bottom of a pond somewhere." I gazed into bright blue eyes fondly. Today she was wearing a beautiful mint green satin tunic shirt with three-quarter length sleeves. Her silky blond hair—a wig, of course—had been meticulously styled and blended with her own short bleached curls. Her cosmetics were a bit overpowering but had been applied with expert care.

"Now, just what do you mean by that that, Miss Denni? I'm hurt." Solange, whose birth name was Russell Otis and whose most sacred secret was tucked between her legs and covered under an hour's worth of padded clothing, feigned bewilderment.

"I worry about you and that penchant you have for the bad boys," I responded with a mischievous grin.

"They're not all bad, honey. In fact, some are very, very good," she joked, adjusting her amethyst bracelet on her smooth, hairless arm. "Some are just that good," she added in a sly whisper.

"Oh no! No more information, please," I said, laughing helplessly and pushing aside my empty bowl. "You want some gumbo?"

"No, no, Emma and I just finished a good platter of oysters and shrimp. So well done here." She paused and watched me keenly with her heavily mascaraed eyes. "What *are* you looking at?"

I blushed, realizing my attention had not been focused entirely on Solange. "It's Yolanda. Patty's partner? She's here talking to someone when she's supposed to be somewhere else."

Solange drew in an excited, scandalized breath, "No! Has Patty hired you to spy on her? Are they having trouble?"

I could see the juicy delight in her face. "Stop, silly. I think they're fine, much to my dismay."

"Then you look at me," she said, tapping one long, perfectly manicured nail on the tabletop. "I get all your attention, please."

I smiled. She always was a demanding wench. "Okay, Solange. You're doing well? Have you had the surgery yet?"

Solange shook her head in the negative. "Oh my, no! Do you have any idea what that costs? It's a hundred thousand dollars to take that little floppy doodad from an outie to an innie. It just ain't going to happen. And all that testing. They make you feel like a criminal. Do you really think my emotional stability, or lack thereof, would pass? I'm thinking not."

She sat back, like the cat that finally got that canary. "I *am* in love, though."

I was not surprised. Solange fell in love weekly. "With whom, may I ask?"

"His name is Rainerd and he has *the* most beautiful eyes. And his washboard belly...I can't begin to tell you..."

I snuck another peek at Yolanda and saw that she and her companion were leaving. The white-haired woman looked back toward Yolanda, and I was struck by the even beauty of her features. Fishing in my pocket, I drew out a twenty and used the empty bowl to anchor it to the table.

"Walk with me, Solange," I said in a tone that allowed no protest.

Solange swallowed her surprise and rose gracefully. "You never do change, darling. Obviously, you're still working all the time. Is this an insurance case?"

"No, I'm on vacation. Sort of." I nodded my head toward Landa and the mystery woman. They were moving slowly through Alabaster Square with the two of us falling far behind on purpose. "Patty has me down here snooping around because someone is sabotaging Fortune Farm. That one in the purple shirt there is with Yolanda, and, as I said, Landa seems to be acting a little suspicious today. I'm beginning to wonder if she has something to do with all of the vandalism."

"Ah," Solange was intrigued. She squinted against the midday glare and fished her sunglasses from her oversized purse. "Who is that pretty, skinny gal?"

"Good question."

We moved along slowly, allowing Landa to maintain a good lead. The two were still talking animatedly, I swore to myself that it was more than I'd ever seen Landa talk, and they finally disappeared into a shadowed alley.

"Where's that go?" I asked Solange.

"It's just shops. But it comes out onto Saint Timothy's."

I peered around the corner of the alley and saw spiky blond hair disappear into a side shop.

"Petit Mal, a hoodoo shop," Solange said just behind my left ear. Though she was just over five feet five inches tall, her high heels made it seem as though she towered over me.

I flattened my body against the wall, studying Solange's long features. "Why would they go in there?"

Solange clicked her tongue at me. "It's a tourist place is all," she paused, "although..."

"Although what?"

"They do say that Genevieve is the most powerful hoodoo mistress around."

"Genevieve is the owner?"

"Umhmm. Curioser and curioser. She could cause all kinds of ruckus at Fortune Farm."

"You got that right," I agreed.

We turned and peered along the alley again. "If we go down there, she'll surely see us," I mused.

"True and there's nothing you can do at this point. Come with me to Ainchez's salon," Solange suggested.

"Ainchez Paulus?"

"The one and only."

"If I do go, can I meet this new love interest of yours?" I was curious about him, I admit. I wanted to compare him to the parade of other pretty boys she had gone through.

"Of course. He is just the sweetest *bebe*. You will love him. Come with me, Denni. You can't be a spy all the time."

I looked at Solange's expertly decorated face and felt nostalgia fill me. What times we'd had—Patty, Solange and me.

"Do you remember the time we were chased from Courtenay Park?" I asked suddenly.

"And the gendarme, bless his fat little heart, couldn't keep up with us?" Solange giggled low in her throat.

"And how many times we've closed Bay Sally's?" I grinned at Solange.

"Almost every weekend," she replied.

"How is Ainchez?"

"She's good. Old." Solange shrugged and fiddled with the strap of her handbag. "I know she'd love to see you."

I sighed and glanced one more time down the mostly empty alley. "Okay, I'll come for an hour or two."

CHAPTER FIFTEEN

Ainchez Paulus lived on Rue Lafayette in a large Victorian-style mansion left to her by her husband Georges, who died suddenly back in '92. Ainchez, of an artistic bent, had, as long as I can remember, daily opened her house and heart to a wide variety of people, mostly the unusual and not easy to pigeonhole types. One could find painters, sculptors, writers, educators and politicians at her daily salons. I was just one of the dozens of young people she had helped network as we tried to survive, confused and mostly alone, in Brethren.

Mounting the six cracked marble steps leading to the back stoop felt natural and soothingly familiar.

"Mimpot, look at you," Solange exclaimed when a small dark-eyed, dark-haired woman opened the door.

"Ma'am insisted I dress for the salon today," Mimpot said as she nervously fingered the skirt of her formal black and white maid's uniform. Her beautiful, black-rimmed eyes darted curiously across my features, trying to place me.

Solange hugged her as we passed by. "Why, you look wonderful! It really does look good on you, missy. There's no need to feel embarrassed about it."

"Hello there. Good to see you again," Mimpot told me, graciously gesturing that I should enter. I'd seen her there many times—before she began working for Ainchez and was still simply one of the guests. She was an artist—in oils, if I remembered correctly. I could tell she didn't really remember my name although she treated me with welcome familiarity. She led us along the lavish, antique-decorated hallway and into the glorious, decadently appointed ballroom that had been filled with furniture and turned into a parlor for the salons. Time had faded the accouterments, but I felt no less pampered by the dimming of the silks.

"It's Denni Hope," I told her quietly as she ushered us in. "I used to come here a lot, oh, about four, five years ago."

"Ahh, yes," she said, nodding. "I thought so. Welcome back."

Ainchez was reclining on the striped satin divan against the far wall, as was her wont. Her tiny Yorkshire terrier, Jazzman, perked his ears and studied our threat potential, even emitting a short warning bark and growl. Today there were only a dozen or so people gathered for Ainchez's salon, or as she called it, her daily forum for interesting people. Seeing so many familiar faces was surreal and gave me a sense of just how slowly things do change in the Deep South. It was like the entire area was on South Sloth Time, which crawled along as slowly as the gators prowled the bayou for a rich dinner. I shook hands and shared brief pleasantries as I slowly followed Solange into the room.

"Denni, is that you? Truly?" Ainchez raised up to peer at me. I was dismayed to see that South Sloth Time would not preserve the regal blond forever. Solange was right; Father Time had indeed had his way with my old friend.

"Yes, it's me," I answered, leaning to kiss the furrowed parchment cheek. "How have you been?"

"I'm an old woman, my love, and that's all there is to say about that. Now listen, you may know some of these ruffians, but you probably haven't met our new parish chairman, Taylor Morrissey. His family moved here from over Beulah way at the turn of the century, but he's been away and then recently returned to take over his uncle's farm out there next to John Clyde's."

I nodded to yet a few more familiar faces as I turned to shake Morrissey's hand. Taylor Morrissey was a large, jowly man, just the high side of middle age, who dressed in stereotypical political style even in the swampy Louisiana heat—a three-piece suit, a bowtie and a colorful silk tapestry vest. He eyed me studiously, as if discreetly measuring my value to his office.

"Pleased to meet you, ma'am," he said.

"Taylor is one of our more prosperous gentleman farmers, Denni," Ainchez added.

"Now, Ainchez, I appreciate the gentleman title, but I'm not so sure about this prosperous business." This comment brought a smattering of polite laughter. "I'm a struggling farmer just like the rest of the community."

"Then you must be aware of your neighbor's troubles of late," I responded, watching him keenly.

"Yes, so unfortunate, a real run of bad luck. I know Dodson Price must be just spinning in his grave."

"Can you think of anyone who would be out to hurt Fortune Farm's business?" I asked.

He looked genuinely surprised. "No, I can't think of a soul. Price has been successful, shipping hay up to Tennessee and Kentuck, and it's food for some of the finest racehorses. Plus Dodson always had a commercial contract for his cane. There's just no competition around here. Maybe up north it's different, but people around here respect one another's livelihood."

"But it was my understanding that you grew hay as well." I had to admire his smooth delivery. He was good.

"Oh no, Denni. His sheep are prize-winners at the county fair. For two years running, I might add," said Ainchez. "Y'all come sit down. No need to stand. Mimpot, bring that lemonade over here."

I took a seat next to Morrissey, who had lumbered over to the leather sofa. Solange sank gracefully into the Queen Anne chair on my left.

"So, sheep," I mused. "I bet the heat is brutal on them."

Morrissey agreed right away, nodding as he sipped clear liquor from an etched tumbler. I accepted the sugar-rimmed glass of lemonade mixed with Southern Comfort that Mimpot offered.

"It is that, but we shear them high two times a year and they do all right. Thrive even, if you graze them properly. This year's been a hard one, though."

He crossed his legs and pampered the crease of his trousers. "How do you mean?" I asked.

Solange stirred, and I could tell she was growing bored with shoptalk. Her attention span was about as long as a mosquito's.

"Well," he said with a heavy sigh. "The grazing fields are off at our place this year. I'm not sure what the problem is. We've moved over to the north pasture and are fertilizing and watering the south, trying to get it back up to par."

Solange elbowed me roughly, and I looked away from Taylor to see a young, willowy, very pretty blond man enter the room. He was dressed in country-western couture, from his pointy-toe leather boots up to his button-down denim shirt. He even wore a bolo tie with a huge turquoise nugget in it. He saw Solange and his visage practically glowed with delight. He approached impossibly quickly, kneeling next to Solange and staring up at her with adoring crystal blue eyes.

Solange tittered like a schoolgirl and touched the boy's shoulder. "Rainy, my darling boy, I want you to meet my old friend, Denni Hope. She's from up near Washington, DC."

Rainy swiveled his head so that he was looking up at me with a beguiling, adorable expression. "Denni Denni. So pretty," he said. "Isn't she pretty?" he added, looking toward Solange.

Solange pretended offense. "And here I thought *I* was your beauty," she chided, pouting.

Rainy smiled and, if possible, made his gaze even more adoring. "Ah, you know it's you, and only you, I have eyes for, my beautiful one."

"Solange, you two do carry on so," Ainchez said with a disdainful sniff. Jazzman begged to be held, and she swept her legs to the floor and sat up to cuddle him closer and offer him tidbits from a small saucer.

Taylor Morrissey shifted, clearly uncomfortable with Rainerd and Solange's cooing and goo-goo eyes. I decided to rescue him.

"So, Mr. Morrissey, what do your other neighbor, the Thibideauxs, produce on their farm?"

"It's Taylor, young woman, Taylor, and I think they grow cane and some rice. At least that's what it looks like when I drive by. They seem to keep to themselves now that Thomas and Dona have passed."

"They say Thomas's girlfriend, Baby Wood, still lives there and takes care of Jimmy."

Taylor nodded as he poured a good bit of his drink down his throat, tipping his head back. "I hear he's a bit tetched. Is that true?" he asked.

I nodded. "That's what I hear. Made weird by his military service."

Taylor nodded sympathetically. "Probably war of some kind. Nothing good has ever come from war, as far as I can see."

I nodded my agreement. "So...Taylor. Have you been approached by any developers who want to buy your land?"

Morrissey swung sharp eyes toward me. "Developers? No. Has John Clyde been talking with developers?"

I was taken aback by his vehemence. "No, sir, Ammie Mose was just telling me that she'd heard something about them wanting land around the Sabine."

Morrissey grunted. "Land here's not much good for other than farming. Developers can't build in this area because the ground's too unstable. Don't get me wrong, I'd love to make this part of Louisiana more in demand, more progressive. I just don't know as we've been gifted with resources that other people might want."

Solange spoke up, one hand still entwined in Rainerd's golden hair. "Developers! Who ever heard of such?"

CHAPTER SIXTEEN

"Denni? Do you remember Clara Whitehead? Judge Whitehead's wife?" Ainchez asked during the conversational lull that developed.

I leaned forward so I could see the wrinkled but perfectly made-up visage of Clara. I did remember her well. She and I had discussed philosophy and religion late on many an evening when I lived in Brethren. Always impeccably dressed as befitted a judge's wife, Clara also had an impeccably educated mind as well.

"Clara. Good to see you, hon." I reached across Taylor's ample girth and we held hands briefly in greeting.

I looked around the crowded room, wondering who else I had overlooked on my way across the room. I saw Myra Peabody, the hefty, heavily bejeweled wife of James Peabody, who ran the discount store out on 82. She was locked in conversation with Tyde Roman, the retired drama teacher from the Brethren Consolidated High School. His thin, lithe form was dressed in tight jeans and a long silky button-down shirt, untucked. Worn brown fisherman sandals covered his feet. He'd grown and cultivated a short white beard since I'd last seen him.

A familiar group of matrons played gin rummy at the table in a far corner. Their muffled laughter and comments helped liven the salon as much as the soft, lilting music Ainchez's stereo system offered.

Other, younger, adults milled about, more than I would have thought proper for a weekday workday, but then I realized suddenly that school was probably over for the day. Ainchez always had a penchant for teachers and students.

"Did I hear you say something about Price farm?" Clara asked, leaning forward so she could study me with calm brown eyes.

"Yes, ma'am," I replied. "They are having the devil's own time. Someone is wreaking all kinds of havoc over there."

"Megs died, you know," Clara informed me solemnly.

I nodded. "I know. I was so saddened to hear of her passing. She was like a mother to me when I lived here."

"A good mother, she was," Clara agreed, leaning back. "Did I ever tell you about little Patty's arrival?"

I turned toward Taylor, and he and I, as well as Rainy, Ainchez and Solange, all watched Clara. We all loved a good story and we could tell Clara was gearing up for one.

"No, ma'am," I replied eagerly. "I don't believe you have."

"Well," she began, settling the pleats in her skirt with busy fingers. "This is how solitary the bayou families used to be. When I was a girl, you often didn't see anyone for months at a time. Traveling the bayou was hard in those days unless you were a man in a flat bottom boat or some brave ones what traveled by canoe. It certainly was not like it is today with roads lacing all through the hamlets and powerboats zipping through the bayous."

She paused and studied Taylor with a raised eyebrow. "Was it that away when you were young, Mr. Morrissey?"

Taylor cleared his throat and re-crossed his short legs. "Why yes, ma'am. I remember coming over this way to visit my uncle driving a four team of horses. And let me tell you, riding a buckboard, even with good seats, all that distance was not a pleasant feat."

Clara laughed and touched her chin as if recalling something. "Indeed, I remember those days. My papa had what was called a Concord Coach. Was a big old thing with padded seats. Originally it had a top on it but it weathered in the sun and damp here in the bayou so Papa removed it and we rode in the open bottom. It was a pleasant way to travel. It might have been slower, but you could see so much more than you can see in the cars of today."

Taylor nodded, and I jumped in before he could lead us farther down the rabbit path of memory. "You were telling us about Patty?"

Clara blinked slowly. "Oh yes. Well, going anywhere in those days was a chore, so we all kept to ourselves and only got together at harvest time or on the church holidays, you know. So anyway, little John Clyde was about two years old, I guess, and we knew we'd be seeing him at Christmas, so of course I went out and bought him a little trifle, a book or some such, and then we all met at St. Michaels, and lo and behold, here's Megs with John Clyde *and* little Patty. She was just a little old wrinkled-up newborn, but none of us had had an inkling that Megs had been in the family way again."

Clara shifted and crossed her legs. "And of course I felt terrible that I had no present for the new bitty one, and I gave Megs a good piece of my mind for not letting word out. Turns out the baby had come a little early all of a sudden when she was visiting her mother and father over at their retirement home in Florida."

Ainchez chuckled and scooted Jazzman to one side. "Well, can you just imagine how her parents felt when she birthed that baby while visiting them?"

Everyone laughed politely.

"How did John Clyde feel about having a baby sister?" I asked, smiling at the images Clara conveyed.

"Well, he adored her, of course. He still thinks the sun rises and sets in that little gal's face," Clara replied.

"They've always been close," I agreed.

A tall, thin man appeared in the archway, Mimpot at his side. It was Judge Whitehead.

"Judge Whitehead, welcome. Won't you come and have a drink with us, sir?" Ainchez said.

The judge smiled and fanned himself with the straw boater he carried. "Well, I do thank you, Mrs. Paulus, but I'm afraid our daughter Freda is demanding we join her at the club for dinner. Otherwise, I'd be delighted to take you up on your offer."

Clara stood and fetched her handbag from the end table. She moved around the coffee table and leaned to buss Ainchez's cheek. "Until tomorrow, my darling."

"Give that daughter of yours my love," Ainchez told the couple. "And tell her to stop being such a stranger."

After the Whiteheads left, a silent ripple passed through the gathering and people began leaving in sporadic little clumps. It was coming on to the dinner hour and everyone was very cognizant of not wearing out a welcome. We all sensed Ainchez's energy was fading a bit as afternoon turned into evening.

Solange, Rainy and I left together. Solange and I had taken the tram to get to Rue Lafayette and after it dropped me off back downtown, I breathed a real sigh of relief. Solange was fine to be around, but Rainy's obsequious, needy fawning had started getting on my nerves. I quickly ran into several stores, doing a bit of necessary shopping, and I reconnected with Patty just before five.

The ride home in Patty's car was somewhat tense. I really needed solitude to think about what I had seen concerning Yolanda and the pretty woman. I recalled everything I could during lulls in conversation. I did not...could not...broach it with Patty, but I felt as though my head was going to explode. The more I thought about it, the angrier I became. And ever more certain that Yolanda was betraying Patty in some way.

CHAPTER SEVENTEEN

After we arrived home, I realized I needed to talk with John Clyde, and so I told Patty I was going to take a walk before dinner. Suppose Yolanda and this thin woman actually *were* working together to ruin Patty? John Clyde needed to know. It didn't make sense, but so much in life and passion did not. It would appear as though Yolanda only stood to lose if Patty's business failed. Unless that woman and Yolanda planned on ruining the business for another reason, to gain something else, somehow.

Were they working for Taylor? A ruined business is a much better buy financially than one that is flourishing. Did Taylor secretly want the Price land? It was prime real estate, worth a fortune by anyone's reckoning.

Maybe Yolanda had grown tired of living on the farm and wanted Patty to move back inland, thinking that scaring her off the farm would be the best way.

But…would Yolanda hurt Kissy, her own daughter? My mind was whirling with theories. I slowed my pace, trying to think this possibility through. It wouldn't do to alarm John Clyde unnecessarily.

What would be a prime motive? I went through my list of the seven deadly sins—pride, envy, gluttony, lust, anger, sloth, greed—which one fit?

The tumbling thoughts were making me crazy. I spied John Clyde's truck parked next to one of the large hay barns just west of the Price farmhouse, so I made a beeline for it.

I rounded the barn's north pillar, and there he was, standing by the tack box. He was so engrossed in what he was doing that he didn't hear my approach.

"There you are," I said as I moved close. John Clyde jumped as if I'd shot off a cap gun next to him. His hands trembled, and the glass vial he'd been holding tumbled end over end into the hay below. It landed softly, then cracked with a gentle fracture. A swampy, pungent smell wafted up to me, familiar, but I couldn't quite identify it.

"Oh, my gosh," I exclaimed. "I'm so sorry."

John Clyde moved quickly, bending to pile hay, glass and fluid into a tidy pile and tossing it into a nearby bin. "It's okay. You just scared me, is all."

"You need help with that?" I wondered what the broken container had held. Had he used farm chemicals to poison the goats somehow?

"No, I'm good." He straightened, wiping his palms against his denim-clad thighs. "Did you need me?"

"Yeah, I wanted to talk with you about Landa. I saw something troubling today."

John Clyde busied himself closing and padlocking the tack box. Rubbing his hands together, he turned and saw my questioning look.

"What?" he said with a short laugh. "Chemicals for the seed," he explained. "I don't want Kissy in them."

He placed his palm against my back, effectively turning me and leading me into the sunshine outside the huge barn door. "Don't turn that discerning eye on me, little miss. You know better than that."

I nodded, oddly chagrined. "I'm not so trusting of Landa, though. I saw her in Brethren today, talking to a strange woman. They seemed really close. I was with Solange Otis, and we followed them until they went into a hoodoo shop in an alley."

"How is Solange?" John Clyde asked. He wasn't taking me seriously. I could tell by the way he was poking his fingertip into the timbers next to me, checking them for strength. I was angered by his obvious dismissal and my voice tightened as I continued.

"I didn't much like the big city look of her. The woman. Do you think it could have something to do with what's been happening?"

"How do you mean?" He moved to tidy loose bales stacked outside against the north wall.

"Well, suppose Landa is involved with this person and they're working together to ruin Fortune Farm?"

He stilled and stared at me. "That's so ridiculous. Why would you think that?"

"Believe me, John Clyde. I've seen it all. There are certain motives for crime—greed, jealousy, revenge—and they occur most often in those who are close, especially those who claim to be romantically involved."

"I don't know, Denni. It doesn't jibe. Why would Landa want to hurt us? What would she gain? What's her motive?"

"Well," I sighed. "Suppose she and Patty are having trouble and Landa is getting back at her for something. Or she wants Patty to move away with her?"

John Clyde started walking toward the truck. He shook his head. "These actions seem pretty extreme for two people just not getting along. Someone's trying to ruin, to destroy, our business."

"Who better than Landa who knows what the business means to Patty?" I persisted as I climbed into the truck next to him. Once parked at the house, I had to hurry to keep up with John Clyde's long strides. I was panting by the time we reached the side door. Stopping there, I grabbed his arm and forced him to look at me.

"Why are you giving me such a hard time about this possibility? Why won't you work with me on this?" I asked angrily.

John Clyde sighed and rolled his eyes. "All right. What do you want me to do?"

"Only open yourself to the idea. Is it so crazy to believe that Landa could be involved?" I spread my hands for emphasis.

"Why suddenly after more than four years?"

"Like I said, maybe there's trouble in paradise," I murmured.

John Clyde watched me a long beat. "Maybe you want there to be trouble in paradise."

I stiffened. "Ouch! What do you mean by that?"

"Look." John Clyde rubbed both hands across his face. "It's no secret that there's no love lost between you and Yolanda. She and Patty did you real dirty, and I'm not so sure you're completely over that."

Fury—and the bitter pill of truth—silenced me for a moment.

"I saw what I saw, John Clyde, and whatever was between Patty and me has no bearing on this issue. I'm merely trying to explore all possibilities so we can get to the bottom of this, which is what I understand my job to be. Am I wrong?"

"No. I do understand what you're trying to do and I certainly support you in it. You just need to be careful with this one, though, Denni. A lot is riding on what you discover."

"What do you mean?"

"Just that. This is important. Be careful."

"But…"

John Clyde walked inside and I followed, curious about his cryptic remarks.

Voices from the sitting room drew us on through the empty kitchen.

"Here they are," Patty said. "We were just talking about you two." She moved forward and took my hand, pulling me into the room. There, standing next to Yolanda, was the thin, shaggy-haired woman Landa had been with at Alabaster Square.

"John Clyde, Denni, this is Landa's friend from college, Bonita Corcaran. She's on vacation and decided to stop in for a visit."

I found myself looking into the most mesmerizing sapphire-blue eyes I'd ever seen. The eyes appeared to smile at me and an equally endearing mouth followed suit.

"Denni, hello. I've heard so much about you."

"Bonita," I croaked, nodding my head, suddenly shy. "My pleasure."

Bonita Corcaran was even lovelier up close than she had been from a distance. Her facial features were balanced, finely molded, delicate. I was fascinated by the tiny diamond stud she had in her nose piercing. Light seemed to dance in it every time she moved. The white layer of her hair framed her face with feathered strands while the lower layer spread like a feathered stole across her shoulders in a shining black mantle.

Bonita reached for my unresponsive hand and shook it, the skin of her palm warm and dry. "Call me Bone, please, everyone does. Nice to meet you finally," she added.

I realized I was counting the freckles scattered across Bone's nose and cheeks and had to force myself to focus and respond. "Good to meet you too. What brings you to town?"

Patty laughed and slapped my shoulder. "I just told you, fool. She's on vacation."

I blushed, yet tried to maintain my composure. "Right. I mean, what are you vacationing from?"

Bone grinned and I found myself helplessly caught up in a joke I hadn't yet heard. I knew my grin made me appear addled but couldn't seem to help myself.

"I'm a cop."

"Cop?"

"From Richmond, in Virginia. Municipal PD."

"No kidding. I'm a PI—well, insurance fraud mostly. From Virginia too…Charlottesville."

"Cool, I've been to Charlottesville lots of times. What's the caseload like there? What are your primary fraud statistics?" She fixed me with a direct, interested stare. I felt her gaze all the way to my feet. A tickling sensation settled right where the toe meets the ball of the foot.

"It's busy. Enough said. But right now, she's the one working on our problem," Landa broke in before I could even decide which question to answer.

"And we think the two of you should work together," Patty added, turning to me. "They always say two heads are better than one."

Bone and I studied one another, eyes surprised but evaluating. Work together? Why not? She had a cop's experience and I had the investigator training.

"It sounds like a good idea," I said finally. "What do you think?"

Bone smiled and ducked her head with a sigh. "Working vacations are the only ones I know," she said with a rueful laugh. "I wouldn't know how to do otherwise."

Landa shoved Bone, throwing her off balance and causing both of them to laugh out loud. "Poor, poor, pitiful you!" Landa crowed. "I wouldn't know how to do otherwise," she added, mimicking Bone. "Oh, please!"

"I was just playing the sympathy card," Bone explained, studying me with those glowing, laughing eyes.

I responded with, I'm sure, a stupid grin. "Hey, I bought it," I said. "Hook, line and sinker."

"Some investigator you are!" Bone teased.

"All right you guys, knock it off," Patty said, laughing. "Ammie's prepared a nice dinner for us and you know how she gets when we keep her waiting."

CHAPTER EIGHTEEN

Dinner was tough but in a thoroughly pleasant way. I discovered Bone was a vegetarian, that she had a cute way of tucking her head when she laughed and that she caused feelings in me that I hadn't felt for a very long time. She was also brilliant; I listened in on a discussion she had with John Clyde about the legal vagaries of shipping hay from Louisiana into other states and was amazed at her broad wealth of knowledge.

"You're awfully quiet," Patty whispered to me, carving off another bite of lasagna with her fork.

I drew my eyes from Bone and stared at my own mostly untouched plate. "Just thinking."

Patty smiled. "Yeah, I bet I know about whom."

I protested quickly. "No, no, the case, Patty. Really."

Patty chewed lasagna thoughtfully as her eyes studied me. "Why do you lie to me, Denni? You know your left eye twitches when you do. I spot it every time."

I sighed. "Yeah. She really is gorgeous, isn't she?"

"That she is. And sweet-natured too."

"And smart, oh my God, is she smart. I feel like an uneducated buffoon," I said *sotte voce*.

"What are you two whispering about?" John Clyde said. He lifted his glass and idly twirled the scotch inside until it was a small, sparkling vortex of gold.

"None of your beeswax, brother," Patty replied. She leaned to wipe Kissy's mouth with a napkin.

My eyes flew back to Bone, and I found her watching me with a thoughtful smile on her lips. As usual, her eyes remained amused. I smiled, unable to do anything else when she fixed those eyes on me. I idly wondered what she was thinking, then decided I didn't much care as long as her attention was on me.

Being across from her also made me forget everything about working on the case. So when she brought it up, I was actually surprised. "So, Denni, what have you discovered? Any leads on who you think might be involved?"

She leaned forward and sank her cute little teeth into soft garlic bread. I sighed deeply as I watched, unable to help myself. She noticed, unfortunately, and paused in the bite to raise her eyes to mine. I know I blushed a deep scarlet color and fervently prayed no one else had seen. I was blushing so intensely my eyes watered. I quickly lowered my face and cleared my throat. Even so, my voice was shaky. "Well, I met the neighbor, Taylor Morrissey, today and I'm not so sure he should be discounted. He seems harmless, but he could want to expand his holdings. He said that he had been having trouble with his grazing lands."

Bone swallowed bread. "Do we have a formal list of suspects?"

Patty shrugged. "Sorta. Denni's been writing them down. We've been trying to see who had it in for my mom and dad. As far as we know John Clyde and I haven't done anything to anyone."

"That we know about," John Clyde added with a sharp bark of laughter.

"It almost seems like someone wants to put them out of business," I noted.

"How many workers do you have here, John Clyde?" Bone asked quietly.

"About a dozen. Sometimes we call in more during planting and harvesting. Why do you ask?"

"I was just thinking that each one of them probably needs to be checked out," she answered, dabbing her pink lips with a napkin. I watched mesmerized.

"Oh no," Patty interjected quickly. "Most of our hands have been here their entire lives. They're family. I don't believe that's necessary."

I turned and studied Patty, my gaze slipping to Landa, seated next to her. "Sometimes family can be involved, Pat. I see it all the time in my business. Family members can do horrible things to one another."

"No, leave them alone," agreed John Clyde. "I don't want to stir up trouble."

"Seems like that's already been done for you, John Clyde," Bone replied.

"Alejandro, maybe," Patty said. "He's new."

I choked on my iced tea, remembering suddenly that I hadn't told anyone but Captain Seychelles about the board Alejandro had found. I decided that Bone and I needed to have a private discussion as soon as possible. I had drawn attention by choking. Embarrassed, I quickly apologized and composed myself.

"I don't think he's involved," I said. "I spoke with him yesterday, and that's the impression I got."

Bone nodded. "Okay, I can accept that. Hunches are good. Maybe after dinner, you and I can put our heads together and look at a master list to see who we should be concerned with and who we can disregard."

I smiled—goofily, I'm sure. Time alone with Bone. It couldn't get much better than that. "Good idea."

Talk turned to Kissy's upcoming preschool enrollment and I managed to choke down my meal, my eyes falling often on Bone's sweet, delicate face.

After clearing the table and taking all the dishes in to Ammie, John Clyde left in the truck, off to Bay Sally's, he said, and Patty and Yolanda took Kissy upstairs for her bath and bedtime story. Bone and I stood in the sitting room, staring awkwardly at one another.

CHAPTER NINETEEN

"I smoke," Bone said apologetically.

I frowned, not sure I'd understood what she said. "Sorry?"

"Cigarettes. I smoke them. I know I should quit...I know. I just...well, I haven't yet." She was clearly embarrassed, even contrite.

"Oh, hey, not a problem," I said, trying to put her at ease. "Let's go out on the porch so you can have one."

She breathed an audible sigh of relief, and I led the way through the front sitting room and onto the large screened-in veranda on the west side of the house.

"Here we go," I said, dusting off the two chairs on either side of an ashtray-bearing end table. "I used to smoke, but Patty made me quit when we were together."

"Ahh, Yolanda said that you and Patty had been a couple. How long did you live here?"

"Well, we didn't live here. This was her parents' house, Dodson and Megs. We lived in town, rented a little cottage next to the Sabine. The lake," I amended. "About five years, I guess."

"Were you here when Patty's father died?" she asked.

I nodded. "I was. That was a tough time." I paused in thought. "I don't do grief well," I admitted.

Bone wrinkled her nose as she lit a cigarette. "I don't either. I even have trouble with weddings."

I smiled at her. "Yeah. I get that. I'm the same way."

We smiled at one another, and I felt an almost audible click. Surprising and pleasant.

"Hey, want a drink to go with that smoke?" I asked.

Bone smiled. "Sure. Reckon they have Southern Comfort?"

I laughed. "Let me guess. Mountain Dew, right?"

Her eyes widened, and she whispered the one word in an amazed tone. "*Yes!*"

I shook my head as I stepped inside to mix our drinks. I brought them out a few moments later and found Bone still seated but with her head back against the chair cushions, eyes closed. I paused in the doorway and studied the intriguing slope of her neck. It was slender and finely figured and I wondered suddenly how she could ever apprehend a bad guy. She seemed too frail, too fragile. My eyes traveled lower, across the gentle swell of her small breasts, which barely raised the fabric of her muscle shirt as she breathed.

"A person could die of thirst with you around," she said finally, not even bothering to open those merry blue eyes.

I chuckled and placed the glasses on the table.

She shifted forward and her eyes found mine. "Shall we toast?"

"Sure. To what?"

She lifted her glass. "To new friendships."

I grinned and stared into those laughing eyes. "To new friendships," I agreed. We clinked the rims of the glasses and each took a deep draught.

"Mmm, that's good," Bone said.

"Refreshing," I added. I looked at her again and we both started laughing. Like buffoons.

Sobering, I sighed. "Wow, look at that sunset," I said, my nod indicating the ruddy, glowing sky.

"I know, I was admiring it while you were inside. So, Denni, let me ask you this." She moved in her seat so she was partially facing me. I did the same.

"Who would do this to the Prices?"

I rambled through my own brain, trying to make sense of the information I had already gathered. "I've been pondering the motives. Seems like, one, someone has an ax to grind, or two, they want to force the Price family off the land."

"To what end, though?" Bone queried. "It's farmland and farming seems to be a dying business."

"True. Ammie, the housekeeper, told me that developers might be trying to put in a theme park of some kind here."

She shook her head in the negative. "They can't really, from a PR standpoint, afford to work that way. Threaten the landholders? I don't think so."

"It's possible," I said thoughtfully. "They could have hired a professional..."

"Yeah, it would take a professional to clock a little kid that way." She stared at the sunset.

"A heartless bastard."

We fell silent, enjoying the fading of the day as well as the burgeoning feelings of attraction between us. I glanced sideways at her and felt a stirring inside me. I wondered if she felt it too. Although I knew it was ridiculous for me to feel the way I did toward her, especially this quickly, I couldn't seem to help myself. She was the first person I'd met in the past handful of years that I had any real desire to get to know intimately. It was puzzling that she should affect me so.

I realized suddenly that she was watching me. Closely. Could she read my mind?

"So, let's make a list," she said softly.

I reached into the front pocket of my jeans and pulled forth a bedraggled notebook with a stub of pencil pushed through the wire binding. It had been obviously around a while and I would readily admit that I felt naked unless I kept it with me at all times. I flipped through until I found the notes I'd made about the Price events.

"After talking with the family and Ammie, I came up with Taylor Morrissey, who owns Mossrock Farm, next door to this one. Also, the developers, as I said before. Then there's Jimmy Thibideaux..."

"Jimmy Thibideaux? Who's that?" she asked, tilting her head to one side.

"He's the neighbor on the other side. Ammie caught him snooping around the grounds one day."

"Ahh," she nodded sagely. "Go on." She lit a new cigarette. Smoke swirled around her like Salome writhing through the dance of the seven veils.

"Umm, he lives with his stepmother. I thought I—we—might go talk to them and see if they know anything."

"Or act guilty," she added.

"Yes." I was having a hard time concentrating on the case, being this close to Bone. I mentally chastised myself.

"Any other suspects?"

"There's Alejandro, a new farmhand, but, as I said, I don't think he's the one." I leaned forward so my voice wouldn't carry. "He was acting pretty suspicious when I saw him yesterday. He'd found the board that was used to hit Kissy. I think whoever did it drove a truck down in the bayou, hit her with the board, then drove away really quickly, tossing the board out the truck window as he went along that main road that wraps around the home site."

She sat up and studied my face. "Seems like we need to question everyone and see if they've seen a strange truck."

"Yeah, I thought of that. The problem is, John Clyde hires contract labor when they're planting or harvesting. They drive their own vehicles." I shook my head. "I don't think anyone would have noticed."

Bone sighed and sat back. "Let's still question everyone. Maybe a description will come through that we can use when it's time to prosecute."

I nodded. "Speaking of prosecution, I met with Captain Armbruster Seychelles today. He's with the Brethren PD. I gave him the board. He said they hadn't found any leads, so he was really glad to receive the board as forensic evidence. He's gonna renew the investigation and said he will be down collecting boards off of Ruddy Bayou, where the truck tracks are."

Bone nodded and crushed out her cigarette. "Good to know that. What about the Morrissey guy?"

"He's a puzzle. Big fish in a little pond. Parish chairman with big political aspirations."

"Could he be wanting more power, like from owning more land?"

"I didn't pick up on that, but that's my first guess. He was good friends with Dodson, though I don't remember him from before. Seems like a nice enough guy."

Bone sighed. "What say we do that Jimmy Whatsit family first? Morrissey could have more to lose if he was found out, so it seems more likely it could be the other guy, since he was snooping around here and all."

I nodded and drained my glass. "I thought that too. Wanna go tomorrow?"

She nodded and her head tilted again as she studied me. "So, Denni, tell me about you. Where did you grow up?"

"DC. On the outskirts. How about you?" I said.

"Florida, but my dad was military so we ended up in Virginia."

"Better than Florida?" I lifted her empty glass and moved toward the door to inside.

"Maybe. I like living there." She nodded to my unspoken question about another drink.

I returned moments later and Bone and I ended up talking about ourselves and drinking Southern Comfort and Mountain Dew until almost two in the morning.

"And Landa? How do you two know one another?" I asked at one point.

"College. She was up at Mary Baldwin. Not sure why 'cause it's a godawful ways from here. She said her parents wanted her at an all-girls school to keep her outta trouble." She chuckled and shifted in her chair. "If they'd only known."

I studied her closely, wondering if she were pulling my leg. "What? Yolanda?"

Bone's eyes grew large. "Lord!" she exclaimed. "That girl was the talk of the campus. She went through women the way I go through chocolate candy. She tried men at first and decided early on that she'd have none of that. Then it was Katy, bar the door."

"So…" I had to know. "Did she put the moves on you?"

Bone scoffed. "Tried! I saw through her games right away and called her on them. That's what cemented us and we've been good friends ever since."

I shook my head and lifted my mostly empty glass. I was feeling the SoCo, but my thoughts were still clear. "I can't see her that way. I admit I was angry when Pat went for her and maybe I didn't want to see it. But later…" I sighed. "Later, we just didn't click."

"One thing I discovered about her, something no one knows, is that she's really shy." Bone leaned forward and captured my gaze with hers. "I mean, painfully so. If she's not trying to get into your pants or doesn't know you real well, she just isn't going to talk to you. It's like she can't."

"But she talks to Patty just fine," I argued petulantly.

Bone studied me a long beat. "I feel bad, how she did you. That was wrong. But they do seem happy, don't you think?"

I nodded quickly, to make up for my earlier whine. "Yes, and don't get me wrong. I am happy for them. I still consider Patty a dear friend and we're putting all that behind us." I added, just a touch of bravado to my voice.

Bone leaned back, her eyes mesmerizing as they watched me. Pulling my gaze away, I looked at my watch. We needed to get some sleep.

"Yeah, we need to turn in," Bone agreed, as she saw me check my watch. She sighed and I could tell that she was as reluctant as I was to break this wonderful connection we had forged. There was a slight chill in the air now, but the warmth of the evening still hovered inside our screened-in cocoon. Crickets still called in the underbrush, so it couldn't have been too cool outside.

"Look, you can see the lights from the Sabine from here," she said, pointing.

"Boats. Cargo barges, most likely," I said.

"They're still pretty." She stood and stretched.

"That they are. Where's your room?" I asked.

"Down the hall from Landa and Patty. You?"

"Off the kitchen. I'll walk you up, though." I stood and opened the door to the sitting room. I escorted her through, turning off lights as we progressed through the house. When we reached the stairway, Bone turned to me. "You go on to bed, hon. I'll be okay from here."

I grinned, feeling devilment swell in me. "What? Nervous?"

"That you might want to come in with me?" She returned my grin. "Maybe I'm afraid that I would let you."

She leaned and pressed her plump, dry lips to my cheek. The touch burned like a brand. My hands clasped spasmodically, wanting to pull her closer. It was too late; she had mounted the steps and disappeared into dimness, leaving me with a sweet, tobacco-laced scent filling my nose and a cheek that tingled where she had touched it.

Grinning like a fool, I stepped into the kitchen and paused for a drink of water from the fountain next to the sink. I peered into the darkness outside as I drank, one hand pressed to my cheek as if I could keep her kiss preserved there.

"I wonder what time John Clyde will get in," I muttered. His truck was conspicuously absent, his usual parking space, easily seen from the window over the sink, empty. I poured the last dregs of water down the drain and moved into the guest room.

DAY FOUR

CHAPTER TWENTY

Beau Chapel was smaller than I had expected. Located due north of Fortune Farm and surrounded by sweeping cane fields, the house itself was not too much larger than a white frame Virginia farmhouse. The name had led me to believe it to be of plantation size and grandeur. The grounds were neat, however, yet appeared tired. I noted some shabbiness and wondered how much of that was due to the death of Jimmy's father and the resultant reduced income and how much was due to the fact that Jimmy just wasn't interested.

"Oh, good mornin', my darlins'. Do come in," exclaimed Baby Wood as she ushered us into the front parlor. She was a small woman and a heavy smoker, evidenced by the smell of the house and her nicotine-stained fingers. She also had bright red hair and heavy, impeccably applied cosmetics. She was nervous, with beringed chubby hands that flitted about like doves in a windstorm.

"I sure do appreciate you seeing us, Miss Wood," Patty said as the three of us took seats on overstuffed sofas.

"Oh, call me Baby, please. It's an unfortunate name, I know," she said, holding up one palm. "But it was a gift from my father so I carry it proudly."

Thick, but tired, satin draperies behind large pieces of heavy antique furniture hid windows, so the lighting in the room was dim. Even so, I could see that the blush of youth had abandoned Baby. Her keen, questioning eyes watched us closely.

"These are friends of ours from the North. Denni Hope here is an investigator for an insurance firm and this other lovely lady is Bonita Corcaran, a police officer for the city of Richmond."

"Richmond, Virginia? Lord, my mother went to nursing school there, something called the Virginia Career Institute, years and years ago. Is that place still there?" Baby leaned toward Bone, awaiting her response.

"Yes, ma'am, I think I know which one you mean. It's changed hands now and goes by a new name. They still teach nursing, though, both practical and RN."

Baby looked down at her clasped hands. "I always thought of doing something like that, but the sight of blood...well, it just sends me reeling."

"Yes, ma'am," Bone agreed sympathetically.

"Miss Wood...Baby. I was wondering if we might talk to Jimmy for a few minutes."

Baby leaned back, a hand over her mouth. "Oh my, what has he done now? I can assure you he meant no harm and we'll certainly take care of any damages..."

"No, no, Baby," Patty hastened to reassure her. "We just need to ask him some questions. Some strange things have been happening over at Fortune, and we were thinking he may have seen something."

Baby sighed deeply and closed her eyes with relief. "Oh well, I'm so glad that's all you need. I'm sure he'll be glad to help you. Let me go fetch him for you."

She stood and straightened her frilly pink blouse over the waist of her cropped blue jeans. "I'll be right back and I'll bring you ladies some iced tea. It's a scorcher out there already today."

After she left the room, Patty, Bone and I looked at one another. "Oh yeah," Patty whispered. "I can see what old man Thibideaux saw in her."

Bone shrugged. "She's cute, in a fifties' sort of way."

I grinned. "All she needs is a poodle skirt. She already has the Keds."

"Stop it, you two," Patty scolded, but she was laughing with us.

A figure loomed in the arched doorway to the foyer. He was pressed against the doorjamb, watching us, but I spied him right away. His tawny hair was long and pulled back into a careless ponytail. His unshaven face was very long and lean like a coyote's. He was wearing jeans ripped at the right knee and a pale blue Led Zeppelin T-shirt. He wore old, unevenly laced work boots, and one leg of his jeans was tucked in, one out. I lifted my eyes to his and found him studying me as hard as I was studying him. His eyes were dark, probably brown, and deep-set. They seemed haunted somehow, and I suddenly remembered what Ammie had said about his war experiences. I turned my head and caught Patty's eye. I indicated the man with a sideways nod.

"Jimmy? Is that you?" Patty stood and moved past me. Jimmy came forward and shook the hand she extended. He nodded shyly as Baby bustled in behind him carrying five glasses of iced tea on an ornately decorated silver tray. "Lordy, I bet I haven't seen you since high school. How are you?"

"Here we go, ladies. Something to pick you right up." She placed the tray on the coffee table and stood back. "Jimmy. Come on over here and let these gals ask you some questions."

She turned to us and spoke as if Jimmy wasn't there. "He's been fishing all morning, a quiet pastime as well you can imagine, and sometimes he plumb forgets to use his words."

"I can talk. I just don't know anything," Jimmy said, but he took a seat in a rust-colored easy chair next to the sofa and accepted the glass Baby handed him.

"There's been some goings-on over at Fortune Farm, and we were wondering if you might have seen something. Ammie Mose says sometimes you like to walk across Fortune in the mornings," I said, watching him closely for some sign of discomfort or concern. There was nothing. He appeared numb, his expression blank.

"He does like to walk," Baby offered, sipping her tea. "What kinds of things have been happening?"

Patty turned to Baby. "We've had some vandalism, someone sugared our tractors, that sort of thing. Cost us a bundle."

Baby drew back in horror, mouth hanging open. "Oh my Lord! That's just a disgrace to all that's holy, that is. Have you seen anything strange over there, Jimmy?"

Jimmy shook his head no, but he shifted in his seat, listing to one side like he was uncomfortable. His face mirrored that discomfort.

"Jimmy?" I asked. "Do you have anything to tell us?" I glanced at Bone. She was idly rocking her tea glass, her eyes fixed on Jimmy.

"Have you seen any new faces on our land, Jimmy?" Patty asked quietly. "Do you know of anyone who might want to harm us?"

He leaned forward and fixed Patty with his dark, spooky eyes. He studied her with squinted eyes for an eon of seconds. "I think you all need to leave," he said in a low, gravelly voice.

Patty drew back, surprised. "What?"

"Look here, Patty. I respect the hell outta you but I don't want no part of this."

"Of what, Jimmy? What is it you're not telling us?" I asked, feeling a sudden wash of excitement that he might really know something or be involved himself.

"Jimmy…" Patty began.

His voice rose in sudden, unwarranted anger. "I don't know who is doing this business to your farm, but you need to look to your own house. Don't come asking around here like we was to blame for your problems. You got a poison over there at your place and you'd best tend to that. Carve it out like the cancer it is."

"Jimmy!" Baby admonished in surprise. "I'm so sorry, girls. He's just…"

Jimmy stood and we all recoiled just a bit. He was like a loaded gun with the safety off. He strode through the foyer to the front doorway. He turned back and studied us. "Look to your own damn house," he said as he opened the door and left the house.

Silence fell as we recovered from his outburst.

"Well," Baby said, her cheeks flaming pink. "I am so very sorry for his rudeness. You know, he was a doctor, and he went to help in that Grenada war and he just never was the same after he came home. There was some kind of blast and they sent him home with his head all bandaged. I guess…"

"It's all right, Baby," Patty said. "I'm sure he didn't mean anything by what he said."

"It was odd, though, wasn't it?" Bone said in a musing tone. "'Look to your own house,' he said. I wonder what that could mean." She was studying Patty.

We stayed a few more moments and then said strained goodbyes. Baby promised that she would tell us if Jimmy shared any information.

"So what do you think?" I muttered to Bone as we followed Patty to the car.

"I think there's a lot more going on here than we know, more than just vandalism," she replied.

CHAPTER TWENTY-ONE

Since it was still early, Bone and I decided we would drive her rental car around the farm and talk to some of the farmhands. We saw Alejandro first and I introduced Bone to him. He was very polite and beamed with gratitude when I thanked him for finding the bloody board and turning it over to me.

"I gave it to Officer Seychelles and he sent some men out to examine the site. You did a good thing there, Alejandro. When all this is over with, I'm going to tell the Price family how you helped me," I said, wanting to impress upon him the importance of being included and sharing with the family.

"That's kind of you, miss. I won't forget," he told me, bowing his head in respect.

"He's new here," I said in explanation to Bone as we drove on.

"Sweet enough guy," she said. "And very handsome."

I laughed. "Hmmm, don't get any ideas."

"Would you be jealous?" she asked.

I looked at her sideways and smiled like a Cheshire cat with a bowl of cream. "Maybe."

Most of the workers we passed were busy running the huge machines that spread this final blast of fertilizer on the hayfields. The hay would be harvested in another month, so no further chemicals would be added past this point. The cane workers were moving the huge irrigation rigs and were too far away to talk to.

We spied a handful of workers who were standing by a truck sharing water from a large round orange cooler set on its tailgate. Bone parked the car, and we went over to talk with them. Several of them remembered me from when I had lived in the area and we exchanged small catch-up talk for a few minutes.

"So, we're looking into some of the troubling events that have happened on the farm here. Do any of you remember seeing any strange vehicles or people lurking about?" Bone asked when a lull fell in the pleasantries.

They eyed her fearfully, shaking their heads in negation, so I interceded on her behalf. "Come on, guys. You can tell us. I promise, no one will get in trouble in any way. Have any of you seen anything? Anything at all?"

One of them, a scrawny young man, stepped forward. He swept his ball cap from his head and shuffled his feet. "I seen a truck, miss. The day the little angel was hurt. I was walking from Northheights south and I seen a pickup that I didn't know. It was blue. A funny blue, like light. It was dented up too. Looked old."

"What's your name?" I asked gently, moving closer to him.

"I'm Luis, miss. Luis Estevan." He grinned at me.

I stepped back in shock. I knew this kid. "You're not little Luis who used to follow me all around the farm when I'd come visit?"

"Yes, miss. And you gave me cookies from the kitchen."

I studied him. "Look at you, all grown up. Now I really feel old."

He laughed.

"So this truck, Luis. Could you see the driver?" Bone asked.

"Yes, miss. He had the pale hair and was thin, like very hungry."

I looked at Bone and she looked at me. We didn't know anyone who fit that description.

"Could you see anything else? Like the license plate?" I asked.

"No, miss." He frowned and shook his head. "He went by very fast and kicked up much dust. I could not see."

"Well, Luis, thank you," Bone said with a heavy sigh.

Luis tucked his head, gave me one more brilliant smile, then rejoined the men as they went back to work repairing one of the big harvesting rigs.

"Well, at least we got something," I said as we circled around and headed back toward the house.

"Yeah, something. So..." she glanced at me curiously as she navigated the dirt road. "He used to follow you around?"

I laughed. "Yeah, he was just a little guy but had a big crush on me."

Bone sighed fretfully. "See? You affect everyone that way. Even me. I'm beginning to think that I'm just like that little boy."

I reached over and took her hand. "Well, yeah. But the difference is, you have a chance."

* * *

"What did you mean earlier at the Thibideauxs' when you said you think there's a lot more going on here than we think?" I asked Bone later that afternoon. We were on the west veranda again, enjoying some of Ammie's mint juleps. A lot of juleps contain way too much sugar syrup. Not Ammie's, though. She knew just how much to add so that the mint was still the dominant flavor. They were delicious and refreshing in the muggy afternoon heat.

Bone leaned her head back and sighed. "I don't even know," she said quietly. "Why would he say that, though? It has to be someone here on Fortune Farm. But then that leads to why in the hell someone would want to bite off their nose to spite their face."

I nodded. "Which leads us back to it being caused by spite or revenge. I had been going away from that some, but this is our first real lead, what Jimmy said, so now I don't know what to think."

"I think I need to go home," Bone said, laughing. "Lay by a pool somewhere and get sunburned."

I was horrified. "No," I gasped without thinking. I quickly covered my emotional outburst. "There's no way I'm gonna figure this out alone and we only have a few days left."

She slanted her eyes at me, not changing her position, and smiled cheekily. "I think I might just have a hard time leaving you anyway, Denni Hope. You've kinda gotten under my skin."

I studied her, my mind whirring. "That's in a good way, right?" I asked as she rose from her chair. "Right? Where are you going?"

Bone giggled and trailed an index finger along my jaw. "Just to get my computer, silly. I'll be right back."

My phone vibrated in my pocket as she left the porch. I pulled it out so I could peer at the screen. Solange was calling.

"Solange, I told you not to call me when I'm with a gorgeous woman," I said into the phone, laughing.

"Ahh, and who is she, *cherie*? Is she as fine as I am?" Her voice was low and sultry.

"No one is as fine as you are, Solange. You know that. Now, why are you calling me at two o'clock in the afternoon? Shouldn't you be over at Ainchez's or playing with your boy toy?"

"Well," she began, "I am getting ready to leave for Ainchez's in just a few minutes, but I had to call you and ask you who John Clyde's little sweetmeat is. I swear she looks familiar but I just can't remember people the way I used to. Especially the younger ones in the families, the kids of ones I went to school with. Today's kids don't look nothing like they did when I was young anyway so it makes them even harder to place…"

"Solange," I interrupted, "Solange! What in blazes are you talking about? What did John Clyde do?" I waited impatiently, my brow creasing in confusion.

"Why, Denni, I'm talking about his girlfriend. Who is she? I would so love to see a wedding in the Price family and I just feel so bad that Megs couldn't…"

"What girlfriend? What do you know that I don't?"

I looked up as Bone entered, carrying her laptop under her arm. She eyed me quizzically but regained her seat and opened the computer.

"I saw them with my own two eyes. At Bay Sally's. I went to the little girls' room in back and spied them kissing in the storeroom. They didn't see me though. Do you think it's serious?" Her tone was eager and filled with curiosity.

I sighed. Curioser and curioser. "I have no clue, Solange. I didn't even know he was seeing anyone and Patty never said anything about it. I'll have to ask her…"

"Don't you think it would be a beautiful thing to have a Price wedding? I could help with the flowers…you know I have a talent that way…"

I laughed. "Before you marry him off, Solange, let me find out how serious this all is. What did she look like?"

Solange sighed into the phone. "Well, blond, with big hair, several years out of style. She was kind of small and had on a uniform, so no clues there…attractive enough, I suppose. Are you sure you don't know anything about her?"

"No, but I bet I will."

"Okay, I'm off now, but call me and tell me as soon as you find out something. Ta ta, Denni dear."

I pressed the end call button, my eyes on the sprawling vista outside the veranda.

"What was that all about," Bone asked.

I sat back in my chair. "It seems as though John Clyde has a girlfriend."

Bone watched me, her brow furrowed. "So? Is there something wrong with that?"

"Well, no...I'm just surprised that no one is talking about it. News travels fast in these small southern towns. We knew about John Clyde and his old flame, Sissie Mawyers, after just one date."

"Ahh," Bone said with a sigh.

"What are you looking up?" I asked, peering across her to the computer screen.

"Land stuff. Public records. I want to see how free and clear the land is here. Do you know if there's a mortgage on the property?"

"I don't think so, unless they've taken out a second one. This land was handed down from Dodson's father, Guillaime, and I think he got it from his father as a land grant."

She nodded as she pressed keys. "Sounds logical. If we find out there's a lien on the property, then it will be a clue that something financial is going on."

"Good thinking. I bet you're a good cop." I studied her profile, wanting very badly to kiss her cheek, maybe even her lips. My attraction to Bone was mystifying. I was not some ingénue and knew the whys and wherefores of romance. This was so unexpected, though, like we were being mystically drawn together. I realized with uncanny clarity that I had no intention of resisting. Universe, bring it on, I thought.

"Hmm? What did you say?" Bone asked.

"You really are adorable," I blurted out.

She raised calm blue eyes. "Thank you, hon. You're pretty adorable yourself."

I blushed and quickly changed the subject. "Are you finding anything?"

She was still watching me, her gaze thoughtful and somehow caressing. I felt warmth suffuse me...and arousal. I looked away.

"It looks as though there's no money tied up in the land." Her voice was soft, almost a whisper. There was a long pause. "Hey, do you smell smoke?"

I raised my head, surprised at the turn in conversation. "What?"

She stood, setting her computer to one side. "I smell wood smoke," she said. "Is there a controlled burn set for today?"

The sound of blaring car horns and men shouting an alarm carried to us on the still summer air.

CHAPTER TWENTY-TWO

Bone and I raced out the screen door and spied a thick plume of black smoke billowing from a large weathered shed about one hundred fifty yards from the house. Several trucks were pulling in around it as farmhands arrived on the scene.

"I don't think this is a scheduled burn," I said as I walked across the drive and entered the expansive field separating the house from the shed. "Tell Ammie to call nine-one-one," I shouted back to her, watching as she disappeared inside.

This was all Patty needed, I thought as I ran toward the fire. Surely this was the straw that would break the camel's back. I honestly did not know how much more she and John Clyde could endure.

"I wonder what they keep in there," Bone called out, her voice jostling as she ran across the rough ground next to me. Somehow she had caught up with me.

"Fertilizer," I muttered, sudden fear constricting my chest. I slowed my pace, grabbing Bone's hand and pulling her back as well. "Fertilizer," I repeated.

As if reiterating my statement, the sound of a muffled explosion reached us and the top of the shed bulged out, then tore free, boards raining down the outside of the building as the rest of the roof collapsed inward. Side panels ripped free and fell with a slow, pained groan.

"Oh, no," Bone said, gasping in horror.

The shed had become an inferno. We were about one hundred yards away but could still feel heat radiating out toward us. Farmhands, standing back from the fire, shielded their face with their forearms. A large water tanker, used for watering the cane, lumbered toward the shed as other, smaller trucks backed away from the heat and flame.

"Oh, God, what a disaster," I whispered. I knew, just knew, that this fire had been set deliberately.

Bone was watching, the fingertips of one hand pressed to her lips. She must have read my mind. "Denni, why would someone want to do this?"

I had no real answers. Yet. "Bone, we just gotta find out what the motives are? Revenge...greed? What?"

She just shook her head. "Some cop I am."

We began moving forward again, loping through the field until we reached the shed's access road.

"I feel the same way," I said, panting. "I keep...I keep thinking there is something I'm missing. Just one thing that will make all the other clues fall into place."

As we got closer, I could see John Clyde and Patty working to pull flaming boards apart from the rest of the building so that they could be doused with water from the farm's tanker. The two were covered in soot. Blackened farmhands were swarming the structure now, using buckets of water to contain the fire. A sharp, acrid smell inundated us, and I pulled the neck of my T-shirt over my mouth to avoid inhaling the fumes. Bone did likewise, and I saw that several of the workers had tied bandanas around their lower faces as well.

Bone and I jumped in, filling buckets from side spouts on the tanker and carrying them to the edges of the conflagration.

Once I got too close and the back of my shirt caught fire. I cried out as my flesh seared. Bone ran over and quickly doused me with a bucket of water.

Moments later, I heard sirens and breathed a sigh of relief. I knew this was more than something a dozen or so civilians could handle. There was also the ever-present threat of another explosion, and we had no protective gear whatsoever.

"Back, get back," I called out to the workers as two long, bright yellow fire trucks rolled to a stop. The firemen swarmed like bees as they uncoiled a heavy hose and fetched tools from the back storage compartments. Patty moved over to stand next to me and Bone as the farm laborers formed a large group behind us. John Clyde stayed over by the fire captain, obviously explaining what he knew about the blaze.

Patty looked gaunt, her eyes filled with grief and rimmed in darkness. I laid one hand on her shoulder. "Oh, Patty," I sighed.

Bone grabbed Patty from behind and held her close, her cheek pressed to Patty's hair and her eyes closed. Tears coursed through the soot on Patty's face, and she took a deep sobbing breath.

"Where's Kissy?" I asked. "And Landa? Are they safe?"

Patty took a stabilizing breath as Bone released her. "She's with Ammie. Landa's sleeping 'cause she has the late shift."

We watched the firemen work for what seemed like an eternity. Dusk was teasing from the west when the crew finally declared the fire under control. One of the firemen, who lived nearby, told John Clyde that he would stay to make sure the flame didn't rise again.

The morose, exhausted group moved as one to their trucks and started heading across the fields. John Clyde lifted himself onto a pile of smoldering, sodden lumber and cupped his hands around his mouth. "Bay Sally's!" He called out, moving in a circle. "Bay Sally's! Dinner's on us."

Patty looked up at her brother, and I saw the first stirring of a smile. Her eyes adored him in that moment, and my understanding of their closeness was renewed. I turned to Bone and took her hand. I squeezed it, letting her know everything would be all right. John Clyde and Patty would be okay and, with our help, they'd come out of all this stronger than before.

Back at the house, I pulled Bone toward her rental car.

"Shouldn't we clean up?" she asked, looking down at her blackened clothing and then toward the house.

"For Bay Sally's? You gotta be kidding me. Do you have your keys?"

She dug in the pocket of her jeans and pulled out the tagged key ring.

"Besides," I added, nodding toward the access road near the still-smoking shed. "We won't get a table if we don't hurry up." Bone's gaze followed mine, and we saw the line of trucks waiting to pull into the traffic on Pepperwood Trail.

My eyes lifted to the husk of the metal and wood building that had stood on Fortune Farm for almost one hundred years. It had stood strong against hurricane after hurricane from Mother Nature, but one man's evil had destroyed it in an afternoon.

CHAPTER TWENTY-THREE

Bay Sally's bar was an expansive but rundown, wooden-structured shack with a large surrounding deck that had been partially built out over the dusky blue water of Sabine Lake. It was a Brethren icon, mostly because the business seemed indestructible.

Originally built by Charles L'Enfant in 1954 to appeal to those involved in the increasing cargo traffic of that time, the Lakehouse Restaurant, featuring traditional and filling Cajun food, had been a booming success. Then, after a few years of waitressing, Charles's wife, Cardamom L'Enfant, fell in mad love with one of the burly dockhands and ran off with him. Horrified that his wife had chosen an impoverished stevedore over him *and* turned her back on all the success that he had worked for, Charles became just a little bit crazy. He eventually hung himself in the back of the kitchen during a busy lunch run.

Deep Southern superstition closed the restaurant for a while until the early seventies when Monty Kennedy, a wealthy playboy from Chicago, bought the business from the relieved L'Enfant children and reopened it as a bar and restaurant called Bay Sally's, supposedly named after a favorite song. Kennedy was a shrewd owner, surprising just about everyone. He immediately hired a young Cajun manager, a woman named Odalia Foret, who, through a wide network of friends and paid advertisements, soon had Bay Sally's as a regular hangout. The days brought the tourists mostly and the nights, featuring a full bar, brought out the locals. Odalia was still the manager and most often could be found in a dark back corner, nursing a beer as she watched the employees and patrons with eagle eyes.

"I really wish you had changed out of that wet stuff and let me bandage your back," Bone said as we stepped inside the smoke- and beer-imbued atmosphere.

"I'm all right, really," I assured her.

I noted that the tables hadn't yet filled as the bar crowd was just trickling in. We walked over to Patty and John Clyde, who were sitting morosely behind matching cut-glass tumblers of whiskey. I gripped Patty's shoulder and studied John Clyde. "Are you guys okay?"

John Clyde looked at me, his eyes cold and filled with despair and doubt. "What the fuck is taking you so long, Denni? Why haven't you figured out who's doing this to us?"

Bone spoke up in my defense. "There's precious few clues, John Clyde. We don't have a lot to go on here."

John Clyde eyed her dismissively. He grunted and took a deep swallow of his drink.

"Let's go," I said, nodding to Bone.

I waved to Odalia and led Bone to a table near the glass wall overlooking the water. "It's quieter over here," I told her as we sat down. The majority of the farm laborers were on the far side. Not that they were a noisy lot this night. I think most of them realized what a financial blow this was going to be for Fortune Farm and their downcast faces and low murmuring conversations reinforced that. They were a messy lot, however, with sooty faces and wet, wrinkled clothing. I realized that Bone and I looked no better.

"And somewhat happier," she added, lifting the menu. "I guess we really do need to put our thinking caps on, Denni."

"I know," I grumbled. I realized that maybe my attraction to Bone had been throwing me off my game. I needed to focus on finding the perp, not on how my heart sped up every time Bone came near me.

"What's good here?" she asked, eyes scanning the offerings.

"Alligator, snake, bear meat…"

She lifted her eyes and I saw merriment sprout in them. "Sounds delicious," she said. "They have anything that doesn't walk?"

"Is this your first time in Louisiana?"

She nodded. "Yep. I like it…a lot. I'll be back, I'm sure."

"Hello, ladies. Looks like you were fighting the fire too," our waitress said as she approached our table. She was unfamiliar to me and I wondered if this was the woman Solange had phoned me about. I snuck a quick glance at John Clyde, but he was still staring into his drink. Patty was on her cell, no doubt talking to Yolanda or maybe checking on Ammie and Kissy.

"Yes, we were," Bone said.

"It's a terrible thing. I'm just glad no one got hurt," she said, taking her order pad from her pocket. "What can I get you gals to drink?"

I ordered a Jack and Coke and Bone ordered iced tea.

"I think she's the one Solange was talking about this afternoon," I told Bone once she had gone to fetch our drinks.

"Ah, John Clyde's girlfriend," she said, turning so she could better see John Clyde and Patty.

I studied the waitress as she walked back toward us. She fit the description Solange had shared. She was a bottle blond, the hair teased a little on top. It was pulled back from her face, but she had short bangs and the bottom of her hair was long enough to froth around her shoulder. She wore a lot of cosmetics, but they were skillfully applied. Overall, she was very attractive. Not my type, but nice-looking.

"I don't believe I remember you," I said as she placed my drink in front of me. "Are you new to the area?"

She smiled, as if happy anyone would show her some personal attention. "I am, but my family lived here. I moved back here from California, Modesto, oh, about nine months ago."

"So you like it here?" Bone asked.

"Yes, very much so." I thought I saw her eyes dart toward John Clyde, but I couldn't be sure.

I extended my hand. "Glad to hear that. My name is Denni Hope. I'm a friend of the Price family."

She took my hand and shook it, smiling sweetly. "Rina Beaudreaux. Nice to meet you, Denni."

"This is my friend, Bone Corcaran," I said.

Rina shook Bone's hand. "Bone, now isn't that an unusual name?"

"It's short for Bonita," Bone offered.

Rina watched Bone for some time, her head tilted to one side. Mentally shaking herself, she asked for our orders.

"This is gonna be a real financial blow for John Clyde and Patty, huh?" Bone said after Rina walked away.

I sighed and sat back. "I'm afraid so. You know farms work on a shoestring budget these days. Especially if they aren't big enough to participate in government subsidies."

"What will they do?" Bone asked, her eyes worried.

"I don't know," I said as I sucked up some of my drink. "Seems like this bad guy may have gotten exactly what he wanted."

"We can't let that happen, Denni," Bone said urgently, leaning toward me to emphasize her point. "You know it's just *wrong*. We have got to get to the bottom of this."

"I agree, but how?"

Bone's eyes widened as they flicked to something behind me.

I spun around and saw the imposing figure of Officer Armbruster Seychelles standing in the Bay Sally's entryway. He was wearing sunglasses beneath his dark blue wide-brimmed hat and even wore a dark blue tie with his short-sleeved uniform blues. Spying me, he walked over, removing his sunglasses. He carried a large manila envelope pressed under his arm, against his ramrod-straight side.

CHAPTER TWENTY-FOUR

I stood and greeted him. "Officer Seychelles! How are you?"

He shook my hand. "I'm good. I thought I'd drop these by, out at Fortune, and Ammie told me where you were." He handed me the envelope. "I saw what happened. Man, this is bad business," he added, shaking his head from side to side.

"I know. Bob Tunney is watching the shed tonight and the fire inspector will be out first thing in the morning. Here, sit." I pulled a chair out.

"I sure hope they find a clue that tells us something," he responded as he took a seat and removed his hat. "I'm getting tired of chasing invisible men."

"Oh, sorry. Officer Seychelles, this is Bone Corcaran. She's a Richmond officer here helping out."

He shifted his hat and took Bone's hand. "Virginia? You're a long way from home."

She laughed. "Out of my jurisdiction, you mean? I'm just here on vacation. Helping out an old friend."

Seychelles nodded.

"Is this the file?" I asked, opening the clasp of the envelope.

"Such as it is," he said, sighing.

Rina appeared at our side. "Hello, Officer, what can I get for you?"

"Just soda water with lime," he told her.

"You won't find much there," he warned me as she walked off. "The forensic guys found some partials on one plane of the wood but are having a hard time matching it to anyone in the system. We'll get there, though. At least we'll keep trying. Anything new on your end?"

"Nope, just the fire. Kinda sidetracked us."

"I did some online searching and looks like the Prices own the land free and clear," Bone said. "I don't see anything that would point to blackmail. We can't even pinpoint a motive."

"Have you heard any gossip about Megs?" I asked Officer Seychelles.

He thought a minute as he accepted his soda and thanked Rina, who hovered for just a bit. "No, can't say as I have. And she was pretty active around here, serving on this board and that. Never heard a peep of malicious news about her." He laughed. "Just about everyone else, but not her. Why do you ask?"

"The grave being vandalized."

"Ahh, yes. No, nothing."

I leaned forward and lowered my voice. "Suppose she was like, having an affair or something?"

He frowned. "Megs Price? I don't think so, Miss Hope. She just wasn't that kind. You know what I mean?"

"Exactly! That means she would have had more to lose if people found out," I persisted.

"How would that play into the events that have been happening?" Bone asked.

I slumped back. "Yeah, that's where I get screwed up too," I admitted. "I mean, she is dead. Seems like that would be the end of anything like that."

Officer Seychelles finished his soda in one long slurp. He stood. "I guess I'll get along. I'll be out at the fire scene in the morning, after the fire inspector leaves. Maybe we'll get lucky."

"You're a fucking jackass, is what!" shouted a man at the bar. We all whirled and I saw it was Jimmy Thibideaux. He was standing nose to nose with John Clyde, and they looked ready to go at it. The restaurant patrons stilled into silence. Odalia leapt to her feet, and Seychelles clapped his hat on his head and strode toward the bar area. Odalia, seeing the police officer, lowered herself back into her chair, eyes studying the situation.

"I'm not selling you squat," John Clyde bellowed drunkenly.

"No, you'd rather turn it into something from *War of the Worlds* instead. I ain't about to look at that all day long," Jimmy said in a low hiss.

"Like you got money to buy. Besides, you'd care for it just like you care for what you got now. Fields fallow, crops failing...all while you fish the days away," John Clyde sneered.

Patty stood against one wall, eyes wide and one palm pressed to her mouth, as Jimmy lashed out and punched John Clyde in the face, sending him reeling. John Clyde fell to the wooden floor and one hand came up to cup his cheek. Blood trickled from one nostril. The fire of fury lit in his eyes and he leapt to his feet.

"What's going on here?" Officer Seychelles said, stepping between the two men.

John Clyde swayed drunkenly, but his hands were still clasped into raised fists, ready to do battle. Jimmy stood back, panting and obviously trying to calm himself. As if suddenly realizing they had an audience, John Clyde glanced around sheepishly. "It's a private matter, Buster. Nothing for you to be worried about."

"Do you want to press charges, John Clyde? You have a roomful of witnesses who saw him hit you."

John Clyde's eyes fell on Jimmy, and they stared at one another for a good while as everyone waited. "No, there's no need," he said finally.

Seychelles took a step back. "All right then. You two shake hands and work through whatever you have to work through, but without fists."

Jimmy extended his hand as his other hand pushed a stray hank of hair behind his ear. John Clyde took the hand briefly and the two parted.

Officer Seychelles tipped his hat to Odalia and left the restaurant. Jimmy was close on his heels. At the door, Jimmy paused and looked back at John Clyde, who was still watching him.

"Just don't sell to anyone but me," he muttered as he went through the door. "Taylor ain't one of us no more."

The buzz of restaurant conversation resumed, and Patty moved closer to her brother. "John Clyde? What was Jimmy talking about? Are you trying to sell Daddy's farm?"

John Clyde was dabbing at his bleeding nose with a paper napkin. He grimaced in irritation. "Hell no, though I should after all that's been happening to us. I hate to admit it, but I'm really starting to hate that place."

"John Clyde, no! Don't say that. Please." Tears made new paths through the sooty grime on her cheeks.

I sighed and pulled Patty close. I so hated to see a woman weep, and Patty, especially, had had more than her fair share of grief the past few days. "Don't cry, Patty. It'll be okay. He's not going to sell the farm." I glared at him, daring him to refute my statement.

"Look," Bone said, taking Patty's arm and guiding her toward the door. "We need to get you home. You've had just about enough of today. Let's get some shut-eye and see if tomorrow will be better."

Patty nodded sullenly and allowed us to lead her out the door and to the rental car. She sat between Bone and me and was very quiet most of the way home. Her breath hitched in a quiet sob when we passed the crisped, smoldering hulk where the shed had been.

CHAPTER TWENTY-FIVE

Ammie was relieved to see Patty. And horrified. She rushed Patty upstairs and into a warm bath right away. Bone and I just looked at one another and shrugged. We were filthy as well and decided our own showers were in order.

Later, dressed for bed and with my back salved and bandaged by Ammie, I moseyed to the sitting room. I didn't want to admit it to myself, but I was waiting for Bone. I just knew she would come to me, and after a short while, she did. She waggled her cigarette case at me and grinned as she stepped out of the sitting room toward the porch. Our porch, as I had come to think of it in my mind.

The night was ripe and rich, filled with the fecund scents of summer laced with the acrid dregs of wood smoke from the shed fire. Lights from the cargo derricks on Sabine Lake provided focus for the night's energy and distant stars beckoned overhead. We sat in our usual chairs, and Bone smoked as I enjoyed the night.

"Like Rina, I'm just glad no one got hurt," Bone said sometime later, when her cigarette bore a drooping tube of ash. She leaned to flick it into the ashtray.

I sighed. "I don't want to be doing this," I admitted slowly. "I'm not sure why I agreed. Family issues are always such a pain. The drama, the confrontations…a pain."

"Some say that's why lesbian and gay people prefer to create their own new families," Bone said. She crossed her legs and I admired the slim grace of her leg below her cotton shorts. "I know why you came here, though."

I eyed her quizzically. "You do, huh?"

"Sure. You thought there might be a chance for you and Patty to get together again. You'd come in like a white knight on your shiny white horse and make everything all better." She crushed out her cigarette and watched me with her merry eyes.

I started to protest. I knew I would be justified in doing so, but the truth of the matter was her words struck a nugget of validity somewhere deep inside. Was that why I had agreed to come? Perhaps.

"How do you feel about that?" I found myself asking.

"Oh, ho," she chortled. "You don't beat around the bush, do you?"

"So that means you aren't going to answer my question?"

She considered my words a moment. "I feel that this trip here was a defining moment for you. You will now either get on with your life or simply decide you can't live without her."

"Ah." I nodded sagely. "I think that has already happened."

"And what did you decide?" she asked, head tilting to one side in that adorable way she had. Light from the lone farm streetlight caught the gemstone in her tiny nose jewelry and made it glow. I fell in love with her at that exact moment. My heart stopped for a few seconds with the wonder of it.

"Denni? Are you okay?"

I nodded. "I'll tell you later…after this mess is over with."

"Okay. I'm going to hold you to that," she responded with a teasing grin.

A sound from inside drew our attention, and Ammie appeared in the doorway. "I thought I heard talking out here. You mind if I come sit a spell?"

"Heck no," I said. "The more the merrier. How is Patty?"

Ammie sighed deeply as she pulled one of the padded porch chairs closer to us and seated herself. "This has been a sad, sad day for that girl. Losing her mama about did her in and now she is dealing with all this evilness. I don't rightly know what will become of this family now."

"Is she able to sleep?" Bone asked quietly in a worried tone.

"She brought the baby into the bed with her. It seemed to ease her somewhat. That other one is working at the hospital all night so Kissy is a comfort."

"Good," I said. "I think the fight between John Clyde and Jimmy was the straw that broke the camel's back. She was holding it together pretty well until then."

"Have you heard anything about John Clyde wanting to sell the farm, Ammie?" Bone asked.

"Can't say as I have," Ammie said with a small shake of her head. "Did he say that? I never would have thought he would do such as that."

"Jimmy seemed to think so," I responded. "That's what the fight was about. That's what got Patty so upset too, the idea that he might."

Ammie grunted and stared at the lights on Sabine Lake. "Don't that beat all," she muttered. "Maybe there is developers wanting to buy up the land."

"Jimmy did say something about the land looking like *War of the Worlds*. Maybe he meant an amusement park..." I mused.

"Wow!" Bone exclaimed. "That threw me at first, but I bet that's it, exactly."

"But that doesn't explain why all these malicious things have been happening," I added.

Silence fell as we three pondered this truth. Tree frogs had recently started up again, and they graced us with a chorus of song to accompany the silence.

I was thinking about when I needed to return back home. About how I would go back to my empty apartment and take up my job pretty much right where I'd left off. Did that life make me happy? Fulfill me? Sadly enough, I was realizing that it didn't, no matter how much I pretended otherwise.

"Well, ladies, I'm done in. I think I'll call it a night. Y'all sleep well and don't let them bedbugs bite." Ammie rose and straightened her shirt.

"'Night, Ammie. You sleep well too," I said.

"See you the morning, Ammie," Bone said.

Ammie went inside and through the house to get her bag, then out the front. She hailed us again briefly as she passed by outside the porch.

"Where does she live?" Bone inquired eyes on the retreating figure.

I stood and pulled Bone to her feet. I directed her gaze with a forefinger. "See that little white light over there...at the end of that short stand of cane? That's her house."

"Oh my, so she walks here every day."

"Yep and has for about thirty years."

"Does she have a family there waiting for her tonight?"

"Ammie never had children of her own, and that may be why she considers the Price kids hers. She's raised them since birth. She had a husband, Erwin Mose, but he passed from a brain tumor when Patty was about twelve."

"She's quite an amazing woman, isn't she?" Bone said.

"That she is," I agreed readily. I was studying Bone's freckled cheeks in the light from outside. Part of her face was in shadow, but her one lit eye told me she was looking at me as well. I moved closer to her, feeling the aura of her essence press against me. I breathed in her sweet, fruity fragrance and felt lightheaded. She moved toward me and I welcomed her into my arms. Our noses touched, then our foreheads, then our lips in the most chaste of ways as we breathed in one another, experienced the spiritual being of one another.

Then, too soon, it was over.

"Goodnight, Denni dear. Sleep well and I will see you in the morning."

I watched her walk away, an ache piercing my heart.

DAY FIVE

CHAPTER TWENTY-SIX

Breakfast was a subdued affair. It seemed everyone, from Ammie down to Kissy, was somber and lost in their own thoughts. Even Human was lazy and yawning. I found myself in that magical realm suffused with the first flush of new love. Nothing could get me too down, although the family's sadness did weigh heavy on my heart. I pondered the future of Fortune Farm as I ate a stack of Ammie's lighter than air pancakes.

Bone was beautiful, as usual, her amused sapphire eyes glowing and two-toned hair lustrous in the morning light. I wondered if she was thinking about the sensual, spiritual kiss we had shared the night before. My lips had now begun to crave hers. Did she crave me, as well? I would have asked her if given the opportunity.

"Patty, can you find the insurance policies this morning? I'll run them over to Robert this afternoon after the investigators tell me something," John Clyde said at breakfast. He wasn't eating much, but strong black coffee seemed to have become the lifesaving ring in his sea of hangover. His left eye had developed a painful-looking circle of purplish blue, and there was a scrape high up on his left cheek. His hair was askew and he was wearing an old paint-splattered T-shirt above faded, worn jeans. Clearly he was not in a caring mood.

Patty nodded. I felt real concern for her well-being. Yolanda had been moved to the night shift for a few days and had not been able to be of much support. She was already asleep upstairs, leaving Patty to deal with the farm issues. Thank goodness, Ammie was there to help her with Kissy. Bone and I needed to have these problems solved before time to go home, for Patty's peace of mind, if for nothing else. Though I knew I was finally over our relationship and its brutal end, I did still care for her. I looked over at her gaunt face and hollow eyes as she picked listlessly at her food.

Impulsively, I reached out and laid one hand over hers. "Eat, Patty," I said. "You're gonna need lots of energy today."

She nodded again and ate one bite just to please me.

Bone and Kissy, who had been working together to make faces on Kissy's pancakes with raisins, bananas and bacon, looked at Patty. I could see concern etched into both their faces.

"Enough of this," Bone said. "The best way to get your lives back to normal is to smash the butt of the guy who is causing all this. It's the only way. I think that Denni and I will work really hard today to see if we can't get to the bottom of this."

"Hmph, about time," John Clyde muttered. He rose and left the room, Human on his heels.

Patty looked after him, a strange expression marring her features. "Asshole," she whispered.

Kissy giggled, and the air in the room seemed to lighten by several lumens. Patty smiled for the first time since the fire, and Bone and I looked at one another, our faces splitting into wide grins. Soon, the four of us were laughing like fools. Ammie came into the room with a carafe of fresh juice and stood staring disbelievingly. Soon she was smiling as well, and she carried the juice to the table, chortling merrily.

"Well, if that don't beat all," she said as she took a seat at the table.

After finishing breakfast, Bone pulled me into the sitting room. "Let's snoop around a bit," she said.

"Sure," I agreed, adding, "you know the fire inspector will be out there. And Officer Seychelles."

"Yeah, but I want to see where all the other stuff happened too."

"Ah, okay."

After donning good walking shoes, Bone and I checked in with Ammie, then took off, out across Price land. The sugarcane was waist high now, creating a striking deep green vista in fields off to our left. Fields of hay, fescue and alfalfa, just now beginning to top with wispy seed, created a lighter green carpet off to our right.

"So tell me about Fortune Farm. You said it was a land grant?" Bone said as we meandered along the dirt road, heading toward the tractor barn.

"Yeah, from the early US government. Dodson Price's grandfather did some kind of heroic thing during the 1812 war and was given about two hundred acres of Cajun land for it. He had the house built and they've been here farming ever since."

"Wow. That's pretty cool, I mean historically and all."

Bone was blushing and it wasn't from the sun.

"Yeah, I guess it is," I agreed, studying her as we walked along.

"I mean, I'm a city kid through and through, and if you have a little acre and house in the suburbs, you had something. I can't imagine being responsible for two hundred acres and creating a livelihood from it. Just seems kinda...special somehow."

"Do you think that you'd like to live that kind of life?" I asked.

She immediately shook her head. "Oh no, I don't think so. I'm kinda suffering Starbucks withdrawal just being here two days. I like the notion of it, though, and am glad it still exists."

I frowned. "I do too, but I fear farmers will become more scarce as our scientists figure out more ways to manufacture food-like substances."

"Eww," Bone grimaced.

We had reached the tractor shed, and I started telling Bone about what the Prices had told me happened there. She walked away from me to examine the walls of the huge structure with its seemingly endless file of tractor bays and I found myself admiring her intriguing slimness. Her body was almost waiflike, but I knew how strong she was after seeing her in action during the shed fire.

"Were all of them sugared?" she asked, one hand resting on a structural timber.

"I think so. Why?" I responded.

"That would take some time, Denni. There's like almost twenty tractors here. Plus he was working at night. In the dark."

I scrubbed at my chin with one hand. "Seems like it would be someone who knows the place. And someone who could take his time."

"Like Jimmy Thibideaux," Bone offered.

"Or John Clyde," I added recklessly.

She turned to study me, her eyes serious and somber. "Surely you don't mean that, Denni. He wouldn't sabotage his own business."

"I don't know. I'm beginning to have my doubts. He's really changed. He used to just adore Patty, but now he treats her like crap."

"To what end, though?"

I sighed. "I'm not sure. Just a hunch anyway. Probably wrong." I paused, then continued. "Maybe he is tired of the headaches of managing this big an enterprise. Maybe he wants out and feels like this is the best way to do it."

We fell silent and moved off across a large patch of scrub land. "Over here is where Kissy fell in the quicksand," I told Bone, pointing off toward the Sabine.

"Can you take me there?" She seemed strangely animated.

We walked silently across hummocks of weed grass until we came to a wide sinkhole. "This is it. She was running with the dog and she fell in. It was terrifying...wait." I studied the surrounding land and realized this was not the same place. "This isn't it. This is another one, a newer one."

"Really?" Bone looked around curiously. "That's interesting."

A sort of intriguing sulphur smell hung over this land stretching south of the Price farmhouse. I had noticed it after we'd been walking for some time. The odor was markedly stronger in certain areas and nonexistent in others. There seemed to be no pattern to it. Here it was powerful.

Sulphur. I wondered if there was a significance, and if so did it have any bearing on the threatening acts made against the Prices these past few weeks.

The search for clues continued as Bone and I walked around several more sinkholes. But there was not even a footprint, certainly not anything that screamed it belonged to the person who was terrorizing the family.

Hot, tired and a bit discouraged, we headed back toward the house. On the way, we stopped at Ruddy Bayou, where I explained to Bone what I had found there. The Brethren police had been there already and had taken the boards that had been spilled along the bank. By the powdery residue on the mashed reeds, we could also tell that some casts of the tire marks had been taken.

"That poor kid," Bone said as she stared at the dark, insidious water. "Glad she was able to get out of the water."

"Not easy with these slippery sides," I said.

Bone was studying the landscape with a pensive gaze. I was watching her mind work. She was calculating something in that big brain of hers.

"What?" I queried.

She looked at me as though I had startled her. "What? Oh, nothing yet. I need to check something. Where to next?"

I took her hand in mine as we made the long walk back to the Price home. We talked easily about our families and the aggravating idiosyncrasies that they had brought into our lives. And we talked about work. She shared with me, telling me about the time she'd been unable to save a mother and toddler from an abusive relationship that had turned deadly. She admitted to the nightmares that had kept her awake for weeks after their deaths. I found myself hating anything that would cause her grief, yet I could tell how important her work was to her. And I also learned about her strong sense of right and wrong. It was that strong sense that led to her becoming a cop more than a decade ago.

"So why are you an insurance investigator?" she asked, trying, I believe, to turn the subject away from her grief.

"Well, before Patty and I got together, I was down here visiting my Aunt Josephine, who ran a little dress shop over in the town of Sulphur, a little ways east of here. She'd just been diagnosed with cervical cancer, and my mom had brought me with her down for the summer to help Aunt Jo out. I had taken my college basics but wasn't at all sure what I wanted to do with my life so figured why not stay with family for a while." I shrugged.

She watched me as we walked a few steps. "What does that have to do with being an investigator?" she asked finally.

I laughed. "Sorry, I was woolgathering. I met Patty shortly after that. She was buying a wedding dress from my aunt, but she was raising hell about marrying a man she didn't love because her parents expected it of her. I was the only one who spoke up and said, 'Wait, you don't have to marry him. Make your own decisions.' That cemented our friendship. We fell in love after that."

I quieted and sighed. "I switched to a small college over in Lake Charles, and we eventually got a place together. I finally settled in to studying criminal justice and forensic science. Just because that's what I was interested in. After we broke up, I moved back north, to the area where I grew up and interviewed around. Alan Carter's firm hired me."

Bone nodded. "So how did her parents accept you after you ruined Patty's marriage? It seems like you had a really good relationship with them."

I laughed, remembering my own surprise when Dodson and Megs had welcomed me into the family. "Turns out it was a misunderstanding of sorts. They thought Patty *wanted* to marry Henry, and they were supporting her in that. They didn't really care. And the whole sexuality issue didn't bother them either. They just wanted Patty happy."

"Wow," Bone said hollowly. "You don't find that kind of unconditional love much. Not what I would have expected, that's for sure."

"Yep, tell me about it." I went on to share my own coming-out story and my parents' reaction and encouraged her to share hers. Watching her speak, I badly wanted another kiss, but I was content to explore her fascinating mind for now. Getting to know the many nuances of Bone was becoming my new hobby.

Climbing the slight rise along the road toward the house, we veered right and ended up at the location where the shed had once stood. Now it was just a blackened shell of wood and melted fiberglass. John Clyde, Seychelles and several other men, most likely the insurance inspectors, scurried about the wreckage. Patty was there as well, and she greeted us absently as we arrived.

"Have they found anything yet?" I asked.

"Accelerant. Most likely kerosene. They found a puddle at the back and also by the door. It was an amateur job, with no effort to try and disguise what they were doing. He knew enough to know that the chemicals would explode when exposed to enough heat, though." Her eyes were haunted as she watched her brother.

"At least insurance will cover the loss," I offered in an effort to cheer her up.

"That's something," she said, nodding.

"Patty?" Bone moved closer. "That storm you had a few years ago, did it do major damage to the land?"

Patty studied Bone. "How do you mean?"

"Structurally, I mean."

Patty gave the question a good bit of consideration. "Well, it cleared out a lot of undergrowth from the bayou, opened up a lot of new waterways. The rain washed away some of our topsoil, sending it right into the Sabine. Why do you ask?"

"Just an idea I had. I'll let you know if I come up with something." Bone looked toward the house. "Denni, I want to do a little research. I think I'll go on back to the house."

"Wait, I'll go with you."

I smoothed a palm along Patty's back. "I'll check on Kissy for you, okay?"

She nodded. "Sure. Thanks. I won't be too much longer."

On the way back we paused to look over the fenced goat lot just one more time. Nothing. Just a waste of time and energy.

CHAPTER TWENTY-SEVEN

I found Kissy at the dining table coloring in a huge activity book. She looked up at me when I came into the room and I could see the keen disappointment on her face when she realized it wasn't either of her mothers. Her bottom lip even quivered before she lowered her head and resumed her task.

"Where's Bone?" she asked.

"Using her computer," I replied. "Can I color some?"

She lifted her eyes and studied me a long moment as if making sure I wasn't going to patronize her in any way. She sighed deeply and shoved a similar book toward me. "You can color in the fairy one. It's got zoo animals in it."

I took a seat across from her and opened the book. Tinker Bell and all her fairy friends had gone to the zoo for the day. Flipping through, I saw that one of them had gotten lost. Her friends rallied and rescued her. How apt, I thought.

I selected a picture and reached for the yellow crayon. "How are you holding up, Little Bit?" I asked. "I know this is a really rough time for all of you."

"Yeah," she said softly, and I watched, my heart breaking, as a tear slid from the end of her nose onto the page she was coloring. "I've been a really good girl," she said softly. "I don't know why all these bad things are happening to us."

"Oh, honey, this has absolutely nothing to do with you. Nothing, I promise. I don't know why all these bad things are happening either," I replied slowly, my inexperience with children daunting me. How much could a four-year-old understand?

"It's 'cause of the oil," Kissy explained, tapping her full bottom lip with the end of a green crayon.

I chuckled and shook my head. "You shouldn't listen so much to what Miss Ammie says," I cautioned. "She does carry on so."

Kissy eyed me with a superior air. "Wasn't Miss Ammie, was Uncle. He was talking with the fat man the day we were at the toy store. The fat man said they weren't going to wait forever, and Uncle said the Price oil wasn't going anywhere. Do we have oil, Miss Denni?"

Sudden sourness roiled in my stomach. Was this insanity all about oil? Greed? At gut level, I believed Kissy. Why would the child lie? My head, however, played devil's advocate, knowing that John Clyde would never be involved in anything that would hurt his sister or injure the family in any way.

"No, I don't think so, Kissy. I'm sure it's just a misunderstanding," I answered absently.

"Aren't you going to color the giraffe?" Kissy was studying me with intense curiosity.

I smiled, even as my mind whirled, and I bent my head over the coloring book. "Pass me that orange one, will you?"

* * *

"It's oil," Bone said some time later. I'd found her in the sitting room, bent toward the laptop open on the coffee table.

I stared at her open-mouthed. "How do you mean?"

"Rita, that last storm, it somehow opened a vault of oil in the soft shale bedrock below this area," she explained.

I sat across from her. "But that was years ago. I was here then and we didn't see any oil."

"Right. But it doesn't work like that. From what I'm reading here, Rita's flooding, when it receded, undermined the bayou and it's been sinking ever since. That's what the quicksand is all about and those little saltwater pools inland. Also that sulphur smell. Oil is infiltrating the land, seeping up from that vault."

I sat back. "Oh, my god. Now it all makes sense. And Isaac in 2008 probably made it worse. So what...you think that John Clyde might be trying to get out of the farming business and into the oil business?"

She shrugged dramatically. "I don't know. You tell me. I definitely think this warrants a conversation with the man. We need to find out what he's up to, if anything."

I thought a long moment as Bone studied her computer screen. "I think we should talk to Patty first. She needs to be on the same page we are about this."

"Okay by me," Bone said. "But explain to me, though, why sabotaging the farm would help in any way."

"So he could give up on it. The business has always been amazingly successful, and I'm sure he couldn't just decide one day to walk away from it, even for something as profitable as oil. Too many contracts, too many commitments." I was angry at the idea of John Clyde's subterfuge. He should have been man enough to come out and admit what was going on.

"Snake," Bone said, mirroring my thoughts.

"You know, I was just talking to Kissy. She told me that John Clyde had been talking to a fat man about oil. I bet that was Taylor Morrissey. That jerk lied to me, as well." I was really angered now.

Bone laid a calming palm on my arm. "Don't get mad, sweetness." She smiled at me in a way that made my anger fade and my heart swell. "We're not one hundred percent sure of any of this. It just makes sense, is all. We could be dead wrong."

"I'll tell you who will be dead if Patty finds out that John Clyde hurt that little girl." I paused. "Or was responsible for it somehow." I was still having a hard time believing that John Clyde was involved in this, though it sure went a long way toward explaining his drinking and mood changes. Probably guilt, I thought.

"Well, let's go find Patty," she said. "I just hope she doesn't shoot the messenger."

We found Patty on the cement steps that led to the side porch. She was drinking iced tea and talking on the phone. Probably to Yolanda. She looked pretty upset.

"Are you sure this is a good idea?" Bone said, taking refuge behind my left shoulder. "Maybe we should wait until a better time."

"No. Then she'd be really pissed. Trust me."

Bone looked up at me, her eyes thoughtful. "I do," she said softly.

I stared into her eyes and felt my world shift. I was in an earthquake, a hurricane, a solar storm, the vacuum of space. I just wanted her to keep looking at me like that. Patty broke the spell by speaking to us. She had obviously finished her phone call. "You guys looking for me?"

I gulped and moved to sit next to her. I took her hand. "Listen, Patty. I know this sounds a little crazy, but we think that there might be oil on your land."

Patty frowned in puzzlement. "Oil?"

Bone broke in. "I did some searching and it looks like other local geology surveys have turned up some oil deposits that were released during Rita."

"Like the quicksand and that funny smell that hangs over the land. They could be the result of oil underneath your property," I added quickly.

Patty blinked her eyes once very slowly. "I'll be damned. I bet that's why nothing will grow in Southland and why that tarry stuff keeps seeping up and getting on our shoes."

Bone looked at me and mouthed, "Southland"?

"It's one of the names for parts of the farm," I whispered.

"Yeah," Patty continued. "I just thought the land was too briny to grow anything. Oil. Well, I'll be damned."

We sat in silence as she soaked the information in.

"Oh, my gosh," she exclaimed suddenly. "We gotta tell John Clyde. He'll be thrilled."

Bone and I exchanged glances. Now came the hard part.

"Um, Pat, hon. We think he already knows," I said softly.

She eyed me quizzically, then looked at Bone. "He knows?"

Bone spoke hastily. "We think he might. Just because of some things that have been said."

"Like that fight with Jimmy," Patty said, her mouth grim. Yeah, she was getting it. Patty was no dummy, not by a long shot.

"He never said a word," she said hesitantly. "Not a word."

Her sadness tore at my heart. I knew how it felt to be betrayed, and no matter what, I had never wished that on her. Especially by a brother, the only family she had left.

Bone spoke with the voice of reason. "Before we get too worked up about this, I think it would be a good idea to talk to John Clyde. Maybe we're wrong."

Patty stood, her face tight and eyes flashing with anger. "Yes, let's just go see what Mr. John Clyde Price has to say about this."

Patty led the way toward the house, and I widened my eyes to Bone as if to warn and prepare her for the upcoming battle.

CHAPTER TWENTY-EIGHT

As we approached the house, Ammie stuck her head out from behind the screen door. "Someone here to see you, Miss Patty." She stood back and the plump, smiling figure of Erica Nance, Megs's best friend, filled the doorway. Erica was in her late fifties but still bore a cherubic round face that featured deep dimples in each cheek and huge blue eyes. Even her hair was styled little-girl long and still wrapped around her neck and shoulders with thick blond curls, shiny and luxurious. To further her youthful ambiance, today she was wearing jeans and a pale green sweatshirt above white athletic shoes.

Erica and Patty ran toward one another and hugged boisterously as Ammie smiled and closed the door, retreating back into the house. Erica kissed Patty on the forehead before standing back and examining her closely.

"You look like crap, darlin'," she said in her characteristic low, husky voice. Some called her type of voice a whiskey voice, brought on by too much booze and cigarettes. Erica indulged in neither, but her deep raspy voice belied that fact. She was, however, outspoken with that voice and prone to calling a spade a spade.

Patty grimaced and tears began pouring down her face.

"Aw, sugar," Erica soothed, pulling her inside. She looked back accusingly toward Bone and me. "What have y'all done to this child?"

We meekly followed them inside. I, for one, was grateful for the cool air that now surrounded us. Erica and Patty were sitting on the sofa, and Patty was sobbing into Erica's shoulder. Erica held her close and patted her back, her low voice a soothing rumble in the room.

"What in the world has happened?" Erica demanded. "And who are you?" she said, eyes landing on Bone.

Before Bone or I could answer, Patty pulled back, mopping her eyes on her T-shirt sleeve. "She...she's Bone, a friend of Landa's. And that's Denni, my ex, you remember her."

"Sugar, are you all right?" Erica asked, her hands smoothing Patty's hair away from her face. "You just let Mama Erica know what's wrong and I'll fix it right away," she declared.

Patty shook her head. "I don't think you can, this time. It's John Clyde. We think he may be lying to us about the farm here."

"How do you mean? Lying about what?"

Patty sighed and turned to me, eyes begging for me to explain it for her.

I cleared my throat. "Erica, it seems that..."

The front door slammed, and John Clyde burst into the sitting room, making a beeline for the bar. He spied the four of us sitting there and slowed his headlong rush. "Hen party?" he asked sarcastically.

He approached the bar and filled a crystal tumbler with several fingers of bourbon. He downed it in two gulps.

"John Clyde," Patty said. "We need to talk..."

"Dinner's ready, y'all," Ammie said in the dining room doorway. Kissy came running pell-mell from behind her, but she stopped perfectly still when she saw Erica. Her mouth fell open and her eyes grew huge.

"Ricky! Ricky! You're here," she cried, running to Erica and climbing onto her lap. "MomPatty said you'd be here, but it's been so long ago."

Erica laughed and pulled the child close for a cuddle and a kiss. "You are just my sweetest little cutest darlin' ever!" she crooned. "I peeked in at you when you were coloring. You've gotten so big and so grown up!"

Kissy giggled and wriggled happily in Erica's embrace as Patty watched fondly.

"I woke Yolanda," Ammie said. "She should be here in a minute."

"Good. Thank you, Ammie," Patty said. We all stood to follow Patty into the dining room just as Yolanda entered behind us. She reached and took Patty's hand, and they shared a sweet smile.

John Clyde held out his hand to Kissy. "Come on here, Kissy. Let's go get some dinner."

Kissy pushed his hand away and pulled closer to Erica. "No, Uncle. Wanna stay with Ricky."

"It's all right, John Clyde, I've got her," Erica said indulgently.

John Clyde eyed her disdainfully, then pushed past her into the dining room, almost knocking her over.

Erica's mouth flew open even as Kissy's thumb found her mouth and she stared after her uncle with haunted eyes. Patty's eyes widened, and she exchanged an astonished glance with Yolanda.

"Well, I never," Erica said.

Once we were all in the dining room, there was a moment of hesitation, and I realized suddenly that no one wanted to sit next to John Clyde and that John Clyde certainly did not want to sit next to Yolanda or Erica, maybe not even Patty.

Kissy insisted that Erica sit at the head of the table in Kissy's usual place, then took a seat directly to Erica's right. Patty and Yolanda were seated at her left. Bone and I took a seat next to Kissy and John Clyde sat at the other end of the table, opposite Erica.

It was a tense meal. Erica explained about the work snafu that had delayed her arrival, but after a long period of silence the only real conversation was between Patty, Yolanda and Erica as they quietly caught up on what had been happening since they'd last visited with one another. Patty also filled Erica in on all the sabotage that had been foisted upon the farm. I saw Erica's eyes slide to John Clyde in speculation a few times—as if she were trying to place him as the perpetrator. Kissy was uncharacteristically quiet and I noted that her thumb found her mouth more often than her fork did.

John Clyde drank, a lot, even asking Ammie to bring the entire bottle of scotch to the table. He ate very little, and his brooding presence made all of us nervous. Bone and I ate quietly, eyes on our plates mostly. I don't know about her, but I fervently wanted to be someplace else. Anywhere but here. My mind was racing, and I was thinking about all the things that had happened here at Fortune Farm. Could John Clyde have actually been responsible for all of it?

After dinner, we faced a dilemma: There was no opportunity to talk to John Clyde. Patty seemed preoccupied with Erica and getting her settled in. Yolanda took Kissy up to bathe her and get her ready for bed. John Clyde retired to the sitting room, opened a book and proceeded to fall into a drunken sleep while pretending to read it.

Bone and I ended up on our porch.

"Well, that went well," Bone said, her lips lifting in a small smile. She lit a cigarette and blew the smoke high. She had pulled her hair back because the porch was sweltering still, and I enjoyed feasting my eyes on the sweet slope of her neck.

"I can tell the Price family is just falling over themselves with worry," I added sarcastically.

We fell silent, serenaded by the plethora of crickets in the brush outside.

"What made you color your hair that way?" I asked.

"My beautician friend, Laura. She talked me into it. Don't you like it?" She watched me with that calm, measuring gaze she had.

I let my feelings show in my eyes. "Oh yes," I whispered. "I like it very much."

Bone returned my gaze with a look that I felt deep in my body. Holding her cigarette away from us, she moved close and mounted me in the chair, her knees at my sides and her form facing me. Her unoccupied hand wrapped itself in my hair, and she bent my head back and laid her lips against mine. I trembled and gasped as an electrifying current of desire forced its way through my body, making me feel weak as a kitten. Her tongue gently licked my lips as if quietly asking permission to enter. I opened the door and welcomed that tongue inside.

A heat grew between us as the kiss lengthened. I pulled her closer, merging that heat into a supernova of desire that shook me. I suddenly knew what I had been missing in my life. I knew what I needed, what I wanted. Bone.

"Ow! Ow!" Bone cried suddenly. "The sucker burned me." She dropped the cigarette into the ashtray and brought her fingers to her lips.

"Bone got a booboo," she said, leaning her forehead to touch mine.

"Want me to kiss it for you?" I asked, my voice husky and low, choked with the desire I was feeling.

"Yes," she whispered. "Kiss it for me."

Her voice thrilled my body, and I closed my eyes and groaned. "Oh, honey, we just can't be doing this right now. Not with John Clyde in the next room."

She grinned devilishly. "We can be quiet."

I groaned again and sighed. "Don't tempt me. I'm about ready to lose it here."

Bone took in a deep breath and her hands moved to wrap around my throat and caress my jaw. Her blue eyes bored into me, and I could see she wanted me as much as I wanted her. I laid my hands against her lean sides, enjoying the curve of her waist as it met her hips. My hand slipped past the gun holstered into the small of her back as I pulled her toward me. She pressed her lips to one corner of my mouth, and I leaned my face toward her.

"You're so thin," I whispered. "I feel like I would break you."

"I'd break you first," she whispered, again making parts of me swell with longings and imaginings.

"Go for it," I told her, bucking gently beneath her.

"Be careful of your back! Besides, I thought you said no," she mused, gently pecking me with little kisses over my face and neck.

"That was before."

She leaned back, chuckling at me. "Before what?"

Surprising me, she backed off and stood in front of me. "I'm gonna come see you in Charlottesville," she said.

"Promise?" I took her hand and pressed the palm to my lips.

"Promise," she responded.

"I sure am glad to have stumbled across you, down here," I said.

She studied me, her head cocked to one side. "Ditto," she whispered. "I really like Louisiana."

CHAPTER TWENTY-NINE

We heard a commotion behind the sitting room door and within seconds it swung open. Yolanda stuck her head through. "Have you guys seen Kissy?"

Wide-eyed, we shook our heads.

"Where was she?" I asked.

"In bed. I went down to get her book out of the TV room and she was gone. Little dickens. Probably in Erica's room. You tell her I'm looking for her if you see her, though."

"I will," I said.

I looked at Bone. "I've got a bad feeling about this. Let's go up to Erica's room."

We entered the sitting room and saw Patty angrily trying to rouse John Clyde.

"I'll go check with Erica. You look around down here," I told Bone, pressing her hand. She nodded and I took the stairs two steps at a time.

I was familiar with the upstairs of the Price home. I knew which rooms belonged to Patty and Yolanda, to Kissy and to

John Clyde, but I wasn't sure which of the guest rooms Bone and Erica were staying in. I had a hunch and tapped gently against Dodson and Megs's old bedroom. Sure enough, a voice came from inside bidding me enter.

Erica was sitting on the bed, in her nightclothes, looking at an old photo album.

"Denni, come look at this. Patty was so cute when she was little."

I walked closer and politely looked. "That she was," I agreed. "Still is. Hey, is Kissy in here with you?"

I didn't want to alarm her, but I could feel the tightness in my voice. She must have heard it. She lifted her eyes and examined my face. "No, I haven't seen her since bath time when I went in to get a goodnight kiss."

"Oh, okay. The little scamp escaped Landa so we're looking for her. Let us know if you see her."

Erica set the book aside. "I'll help, Denni." She shrugged into her robe and followed me out of the room.

"I'll start over here," I said. "Can you start with Patty's room?"

Erica nodded.

I tapped on John Clyde's bedroom door and then entered. His was a typical man's bedroom, with heavy dark furniture and deep, rich colors. I passed through into his bathroom and peered into the shower area. "Kissy? Are you in here, baby? You're scaring us a bit and you need to come out now," I said lightly. "Kissy?"

I noticed that the sound of the crickets seemed mighty loud and finally realized that he'd left one side of his French doors open.

"Like mosquitoes much?" I said as I stuck my head out looking for Kissy. There was a small balcony outside his room with no place for anyone to hide. I slid the door most of the way closed, just to make the invasion of a flying vampire horde less likely.

I moved back into the hall and tapped on the next door. There was no answer, so I opened it cautiously and went in. It was Bone's room, one furnished in light pine and with a floral bedspread. I recognized the distressed jeans and short T-shirt that she had worn the day before. I picked the items up off the back of the Queen Anne chair to the right of the bed and pressed my face into them. I inhaled her distinctive fruit and tobacco smell.

Kissy, I reminded myself. Find Kissy.

Reluctantly, I replaced the clothing and patrolled the room. I checked the bathroom, absently caressing the long nightshirt hanging on the back of the door. I looked with some curiosity over her cosmetics and toiletries, poking at the stuffed hoodoo doll she'd probably bought as a souvenir when she'd ducked in Petit Mal while in Brethren. I looked in the shower area and then moved back into the bedroom. I checked under the bed because it was exceptionally high and opened the wardrobe where she had hung a jacket and placed a pair of boots. There was no sign of Kissy.

Sighing, I left the room and ran into Erica as she came out of Patty's room. I eyed her questioningly, and she shook her head, catching her bottom lip between her teeth. We went into the bathroom together, a bathroom still muggy and damp from Kissy's bath. Her toys, a bedraggled Barbie, some plastic rings, a faded yellow and red duck and some kind of cell telephone toy with bright buttons lay drying on the side of the tub. A sob escaped Erica, and I quickly ushered her out and down the hall, pausing briefly to peek into a shallow linen closet.

Downstairs, I met Patty's hopeful gaze. I shook my head and watched as tears welled in her eyes. Yolanda drew her close.

John Clyde scowled and moved into the front hall. "Katherine Grace Price!" he bellowed. "You'd better come here right this minute!"

We heard no giggle, no call, only an uncomfortable silence. I endured it as long as I could.

"John Clyde. Did you leave your French doors open?"

He scowled at me. "Of course not. Do I look stupid?"

"Oh, hell," I muttered, taking out my phone. I had entered Officer Seychelles's cell number in earlier in the week and I pressed the call button now. Bone was holding a tearful Ammie, and Patty and Yolanda were clinging to Erica.

He answered on the third ring. "Miss Hope?"

"I'm sorry for bothering you this late, Officer...Buster, but Kissy, the little Price girl has gone missing. We can't find her anywhere, and there was a balcony door open. I...we think it looks a little suspicious."

Seychelles didn't even hesitate, something I was keenly grateful for. "I'll be right there, Miss Hope, and I'll send a patrol car over right away. Keep looking and let me know if she turns up."

"Thank you, we'll do that." I pressed the end call button and took a deep, shaky breath.

We all turned as one unit when the doorbell rang. I realized then that all seven of us, plus Human, were huddled together in one mass, seeking comfort, I supposed.

"It couldn't be them already," Erica said in a low voice.

"Maybe it's Kissy," Patty cried.

"No," Yolanda said regretfully. "She can't reach the bell."

I broke away and walked to the front door. The others moved to stand in the sitting room doorway so they could see the front door.

The doorbell sounded again just as I opened it.

CHAPTER THIRTY

"Hello, Rina," I said, surprise evident in my voice.

"Hello…Denni, was it? I'm looking for John Clyde. Is he here?" Rina still had on her waitress uniform, but she wore a long raincoat over it.

I backed away from the door, gesturing her inside. I turned and looked at the crowd as John Clyde broke free. "Rina. What are you doing here?"

He hustled her into the dining room, and I moved back to stand with the others. Muffled words reached us, but I couldn't make them out. A low moan sounded behind me, and I turned to find Patty a quaking wreck. Obviously it had just dawned on her anew that Kissy could be in serious trouble. The other women surrounded her with huge reassuring promises. I looked at Bone, and a sudden thought occurred to me. I pushed toward the group.

"Yolanda, what happened to Kissy's birth parents?"

From the corner of my eye, I saw Bone's eyes widen and her subtle nod of approval.

Yolanda looked at me with vacant eyes. I waited while they cleared and she comprehended my question.

"Her birth parents? No one knows who the father is, but her mother moved north to South Dakota to be with her family. Kissy was in a foster home for a couple years before we got her."

"Do you think maybe her mother...or the foster couple could have come after her?" I asked this of Yolanda quietly, but Patty heard, of course. Her eyes rolled wildly and she moaned again. I worried for a moment she might faint.

"No, no," Yolanda protested, shaking her head. "They had like a zillion other kids. I don't think they were too emotionally vested in her. Her birth mother..." She shrugged helplessly. "I don't really know. I do know the adoption records were sealed. She'd have a hell of a time finding out where Kissy went."

I spoke soothingly to Patty to calm her and Yolanda pulled her close.

John Clyde appeared in the doorway. He looked haggard.

"John Clyde, what's happened?" Erica said, gasping at his appearance.

John Clyde staggered to the sofa and slumped down, head in his hands. "It's all my fault," he muttered.

The room fell silent. Rina appeared in the doorway as huge wracking sobs broke loose from John Clyde. "Oh, Kissy, Kissy," he moaned.

Patty cried out in renewed anguish and buried her face in Yolanda's shoulder.

I turned to Rina. "What has he done?" I asked.

Rina, using her palms, swiped at the tears smudging her face. "I think it's Rainerd...my brother," she said haltingly. "I don't want to believe it but...he said some things this evening..."

"What? What did he say," Bone asked, pushing her way through the others to stand in front of Rina.

Rina looked beyond Bone. "John Clyde," she sobbed. "Tell them."

John Clyde sat back, sprawling across the back of the sofa, his face a mass of tears and nasal mucous. He didn't even bother to wipe any of it away. He rolled his head from side to side, still sobbing.

Surprising all of us, Patty broke free of Yolanda and leapt upon her brother. She started pummeling him with her fists about the face and shoulders. He didn't raise his arms to defend himself at all, just sobbed as she rained blows on him.

"Where the fuck is she, you bastard! What have you done? I swear if anything has happened to that child, I will never speak to you again as long as I live," she spat out, her face inches from his.

I rushed to pull Patty back. "Let him talk, hon, let him talk." I handed her off to Yolanda and Erica, and I sat next to John Clyde. He had rolled to one side and pulled his knees up into a fetal curl. I pushed the knees down. "Talk!" I demanded.

He pulled up his T-shirt and mopped at his face. He rose suddenly and strode to the bar where he poured himself a healthy shot of whiskey. He downed it, then used his shoulder to mop at his face one more time. We could see him mentally fortify himself.

"Somebody better start talking soon or I'm gonna start beating some heads," Ammie growled. "What have you done, boy?"

John Clyde took a deep breath. "After Mama died, I spent a lot of time in her room. Just rocking and remembering her. One day, when I was in there, I saw an unusual-looking book on her shelf. I looked at it for a day or two, not taking time to check it out. Then one day, I did."

"And...?" I asked. I noticed Erica had a funny look on her face. A look of realization.

"It was her journal. Mama's journal."

Patty gasped. "She had a journal? Why didn't you tell me?"

The look that he shot her was pure malice. "Maybe there's things in there that I didn't want you to know. Maybe you don't *deserve* to know!"

"John Clyde, stop it," Erica said quietly. Her head was lowered, and her breathing seemed labored.

"And you," he sneered. "How could you lie to all of us this way? Pretend. For her. Or maybe for your own benefit. Does Clayton know? Or are you lying to him too?"

Erica stepped forward and slapped John Clyde's face hard enough to send him spinning. "You disrespectful coward," she said, stepping back and covering her mouth as if surprised by her own action.

Rina stepped forward and spoke loudly. "You're adopted, Patty. Erica is your real mother."

CHAPTER THIRTY-ONE

Human's whining yawn was the only sound in the room for more than a minute as we all digested Rina's words.

Patty looked toward Erica with wide eyes. "What? What are you all talking about?"

John Clyde poured another drink. "It's true, Patty. They've been lying to us all these years. They…colluded, the two of them." He looked at Erica and sneered.

Patty laid one hand on Yolanda's arm as if seeking support. "Erica?"

I reached for Bone's hand and clasped it tightly. We moved to stand closer together.

Erica took a deep breath. "I was in college…and we were so in love. Your mother…Megs…we were so close then. She knew everything and then when we…Tony and I had a car accident. A huge truck slid…the driver was drinking." Her eyes closed. "There was so much blood," she whispered. "So much. Megs and Dodson came to the hospital and they told me I was pregnant and that Tony, well, that Tony was gone."

She paused and sank slowly into one of the easy chairs.

Ammie strode to the bar and searched through the bottles there, looking for brandy, I was sure. She found the rotund little bottle and poured out a small amount. She carried the glass to Erica and held it to her lips until she took a swallow. Erica sputtered and coughed, but the spirit seemed to revive her somewhat and she nodded her gratitude to Ammie.

"Ammie knew," I muttered to Bone.

Erica cleared her throat and continued as Patty took a seat in the chair next to her. Patty's face was sorrowful, as if she too were reliving Erica's pain.

"After that, life soured for a while, just wasn't worth living. I couldn't even find joy knowing I was carrying his child." Her eyes lifted to Patty as if in apology. "I think I hated you for a while, because I wanted him instead of you."

"And Mama? Megs?" Patty asked.

"She was by my side every day. I dropped out of college, but she came to see me every single day. She brought me groceries and cleaned my apartment. I'd broken my leg in the crash, and she helped me get around. I would have been lost without her. Her and Ammie."

All eyes turned to focus on Ammie. John Clyde made a small grunting noise. Ammie's cheeks flushed in embarrassment, but she held her chin just a little higher.

"Ammie? You knew?" Patty asked.

Ammie stirred fretfully and moved back toward the bar. She didn't say a word, just stared out the window, lost in reverie.

"So for seven months I lived without living, seeing only Megs and Ammie. And Dodson, sometimes. I never told my parents. I just couldn't face them so I pretended everything was fine. Toward the end, I just avoided them. Then it was time, late summer, and I went into labor. Megs took me to the hospital, Ammie was with John Clyde, and then there you were, just as pretty as a picture." She gave Patty a fragile smile. "You had Tony's face, so dark, so handsome. Every time I looked at you, it hurt me so badly…"

"So Mama took me home…" Patty mused.

"And passed you off as my sister," John Clyde said loudly. "She lied to everyone."

Erica whirled to face him. "She *is* your sister, John Clyde. Dodson and Megs adopted her legally after about a month. I saw how happy they were. Megs and Dodson had been trying for another child for almost a year but weren't having much luck."

She turned back to Patty. "You made their life complete. The four of you were such a beautiful family, and I was still a wreck. My life was careening out of control, and I knew I needed to leave this area. Megs took me to a new college in south Florida. She had you with us, hoping, I think, that I might change my mind."

"Tell about the promise," Ammie said quietly.

"A promise?" Patty echoed. "What promise?"

"That I would always stay part of your life. And I have," she smiled tremulously. Patty covered Erica's hands with hers, and they gazed into one another's eyes.

"What bullshit!" John Clyde exclaimed. "The fact of the matter is, you and my entire family," his eyes flicked to Ammie, "have been lying to Patty and me for our whole lives. How do you justify something like that. My mother was a liar…"

Before he could utter another word, Ammie strode forward and bapped him on the back of his head. She grasped his chin in her palm and I could see white flesh beneath her fingers, she was grasping him so hard. "Your mother was a saint, John Clyde Price. I don't want to *ever* hear you say another word against her. Not *one word! Ever*."

She let his face go with a definitive snap. John Clyde had the sense to keep quiet. No one made Ammie mad. He fingered his jaw, eyes downcast.

"So you're my mother, my birth mother," Patty said wonderingly.

The doorbell rang, stirring us from the realm of the past and back into the present with a harsh jolt.

"Kissy," Patty gasped and leapt up to answer the door.

Officer Buster Seychelles filled the entire doorframe, and he even ducked his head as he stepped inside. "Has she turned up yet?" he asked immediately.

Patty shook her head in the negative as she closed the door.

"I shone the spotlight into the brush coming up the road," he said as he extended his hand. "I found this, on the road. Don't know if it means anything though."

There resting in his hand was a very familiar turquoise bolo tie. I wracked my brain trying to think where I'd seen it.

Rina rushed forward and snatched it from the officer's hand. "That belongs to Rainerd," she cried and began sobbing anew. "How could he do this?"

I gasped, and Bone touched my arm, watching me with a worried gaze. "That belongs to Solange's boy toy," I whispered.

"Do you think she's okay?" she asked urgently.

I grabbed my cell phone and found her number.

"Is there something you need to tell me about this, miss?" Seychelles asked, watching Rina closely.

I breathed a sigh of relief when Solange answered. "Denni Hope, do you have any idea what time it is? Why are you calling me, rousing me from my beauty sleep? This had better be important."

"It is, Solange. Is Rainerd with you?"

"Oh no," she sighed dramatically. "I've just decided he is not the one for me. We had an awful fight, and he, well, he *hit* me, Denni. Now, you know I just won't tolerate such a thing. I mean a little play slap is one thing but not in anger, no never in…"

"Do you know where he is, Solange?" I broke in impatiently.

Seychelles and Rina were watching me hopefully.

Solange fell silent, as if suddenly realizing my call could be important. "Why, no, I'm sorry, Denni. I just don't know. He said he lived in a little fleabag place over on Abbott, but I never went there."

"Do you know the address?"

"No, no, I don't, but Lanai's Chips is on the corner. That's where I would pick him up usually."

"Okay, thanks, Solange. I'll call you later." I hung up on her protestations.

CHAPTER THIRTY-TWO

"Hey now, what's this all about?" Seychelles asked, scowling.

Rina sighed as if she had accepted that further doubt was futile. "It's my twin brother, Rainerd. See, sometimes I would tell him stuff John Clyde and I would talk about when...well, when we were together. It was usually to show Rainerd how other people could overcome bad things in their life. He's had a terrible problem with drugs, and it caused him to do some mighty bad things...when he was younger."

John Clyde grunted. "I didn't even know she had a brother and we've been seeing one another since before Mama died."

Rina nodded and looked at him, eyes pleading for understanding. "I've been a little ashamed of him but, well, I didn't want him to affect our new relationship. I wanted to see where it was going before I told you about him, John Clyde. That's all. I wasn't really hiding him from you."

"So what did you tell him and what happened after you told him these things?" Seychelles asked, bringing Rina back to her original topic.

"Well, John Clyde had been really upset about finding out his sister was adopted and said he hated the fact that she got just as much of the property as he did, a full half, when Mrs. Price died. He was all tore up about how everyone had lied to him. He went on and on about it one day, and I asked why he didn't just sell out and move away."

She paused and her eyes filled with tears. "I think Rainerd may have heard us because that's when all the bad stuff started happening. John Clyde would tell me about it and it sounded like someone wanted to make him sell out or make his business fail, so I had my suspicions. When I told my brother what had been happening...well, he looked kind of...I don't know, excited, maybe."

I stepped forward. "So you think maybe he was the one sabotaging everything, writing on the vault, attacking Kissy, sugaring the tractors, poisoning the goats, burning the shed?"

She nodded, wiping tears away.

"I wrote on the vault," John Clyde said dully. "I was drunk and angry. I did that and..." He took a deep breath and his eyes flicked to Patty. "I pawned away Mama's jewelry so Patty wouldn't get it. But nothing else."

I closed my eyes. How convoluted could this get?

"So, wait. Do you think he would hurt Kissy again? Do you think he has her?" Patty asked, running forward and pulling Yolanda behind her. "We need to find him. Take us to him."

Rina shook her head. "I went by there, where he lives. He wasn't home."

Seychelles sighed and pulled out a small notebook as his radio squawked. "Where does he live, miss? And tell me your full name."

Rina complied as I studied the faces around us. Ammie was hugging herself and looking out the window. I thought she might be praying. Human had curled up in a little ball in one corner and was watching all of us with questioning eyes. Patty and Yolanda stood in the middle of the foyer, grasping one another's hands, their faces sorrowful and afraid. Erica sat in an easy chair, studying her hands and spinning her wedding ring, and Bone stood behind the sofa. She was watching John Clyde. He was drinking again, sitting on one of the barstools. Rina and Seychelles stood in the doorway talking quietly. The image of this room, this tableau of misery, would be forever burned into my memory.

Suddenly, without warning, Patty erupted again. She stepped over and slapped the tumbler from John Clyde's hands, and it flew across the room, turning end over end but not spilling any of its amber contents until it crashed into the wall next to the heavy draperies covering the huge picture window. Golden whiskey and glass shards rained down the wallpaper.

"Why can't you be a man?" she hissed. "Go on out there and find your niece instead of sitting here getting drunk *again*. I swear, John Clyde, I'm beginning to be glad there's none of your genetic material in me. I've never known you to be so weak. So, so *pathetic!*"

"Here now, that's not gonna help anything," Officer Seychelles said in a low, sympathetic voice. "My men are pulling in the drive now, and we're gonna start looking for your little girl. She's probably just wandered off. Kids do that all the time."

"Not at night," Patty said tearfully. "Not Kissy. She sleeps with a nightlight on all the time. She's...she's a-a-afraid of the dark!" She and Yolanda sobbed together quietly as they held one another.

"So, how do we find her? What's the procedure here?" I asked Officer Seychelles.

He straightened his uniform tool belt and sighed. "Well, when the men get here, we'll search in three-foot grids all across each acre. Only the ones around the house here. She's a bitty thing and couldn't have wandered very far. We'll concentrate on the river and the bayou too. In case she wandered in there."

"What about Rainerd? What will we do about him? Suppose he took her off somewhere?" Bone asked.

Officer Seychelles shook his head. "We'll search first, then cross that bridge when we have to. You've got no real proof he took her. Miss Beaudreaux is not even sure."

"What about the tie?" I asked.

He raised one eyebrow and looked at me. As if I should have known better.

"I know, I know," I said, sighing heavily. "Circumstantial."

The sound of slamming car doors drew our attention to the front door. Officer Seychelles went out on the porch and spoke with the handful of police officers gathering there. The circling, flashing cruiser lights shone regularly in the front foyer through the open door, making the scene colorfully surrealistic.

I walked over to the door and saw that four cruisers were parked outside, engines still running. Their occupants were gathered around Seychelles, and he was gesturing forcefully as if marking off quadrants of land with his arms. As I watched, two policemen got in their cruiser and drove quickly out of the drive. Other officers moved to their vehicles and started unpacking items from the trunks.

Officer Seychelles left the small clump of remaining policemen and came back inside.

"Okay, everyone. Listen up. We would like for all of you to get dressed because we're gonna need each and every one of you to walk the land with us. We have some volunteers, but we want to comb the area thoroughly. Please, gather all the flashlights you can get together, and let's go find that little girl."

CHAPTER THIRTY-THREE

Looking for a four-year-old little girl on a two hundred-acre farm was very much like looking for a needle in a haystack. After dressing for the outdoors and gathering what flashlights we could find, the eight of us filed outside to stand by the parked police cruisers, their red and blue lights sweeping the front yard with mournful regularity. Seychelles had radioed in to send a cruiser over to Rainerd's home, and we eagerly awaited their answer. It came back about ten minutes later. Rainerd—and Kissy—were not at the Abbott Street location.

Patty had found a new strength now that she felt she knew the identity of the enemy. She had pulled on her hiking boots and stood stirring anxiously, prepared to fight to find her daughter. Erica had changed too and now wore heavy jeans and a denim shirt over a white T-shirt.

The police staff immediately began setting up a command center, even though it was the middle of the night. I feel like they may have hesitated in a normal missing child case, but because Rainerd was likely involved, they worked with some urgency. Additional officers and volunteer deputies were arriving, more every half hour. Soon we had more than twenty-five people gathered, flashlights in hand. Seychelles warned us to watch out for snakes and alligators, then divided us up into two groups of ten and spread us out over the cane and hay fields. If we happened to stumble across Kissy, we were told to shout the word "safe" repeatedly at the top of our lungs and wave our flashlight until Seychelles found us.

Bone and I headed in a slanting course, heading to the left, beyond the main entrance to Fortune Farm. We walked about ten feet apart and we could hear everyone calling out Kissy's name every few minutes. The night was filled with the swath of flashlights, like so many huge fireflies, and the buzz of mosquitoes and June bugs was loud and annoying as they followed us.

"Denni?" Bone called out some time later.

"Yeah?"

"Did you even guess that Megs wasn't Patty's birth mother?" The question was tentative, thoughtful.

I shook my head, even though I knew she couldn't see me. "No, no clue. I knew Patty never looked like her, but John Clyde doesn't so much either."

She grunted. "Wouldn't that just smoke John Clyde's ass if he found out that he was adopted as well?"

I smiled. "Now that would be awesome," I replied.

The section of land we were traversing sloped gently downward, and we quieted to be better able to navigate in the tricky lighting. The night was dark due to a heavy cloud cover, so I was not surprised when I stopped just short of stepping in a small creek, one of the smaller branches of the Sabine. Frustrated, panting and sweating in the heavy still air, I looked over at Bone. "Watch out! There's water here."

She slowed and swung her flashlight in a wide arc. "Guess we'll have to detour one way or the other. Which is best?"

I looked around, trying to map out the terrain in my mind. I vaguely remembered where the main road was. "Let's go left. I think it'll circle around."

Bone walked over to be closer to me, and we started moving toward the firmer land above the waterway. We were met with thick underbrush and found there was no way we could push through. I sat down on the marshy ground and buried my face in my arms. I wanted to cry, but I think there's a point we get to when tears just can't express the sadness and anguish we feel. I wanted Megs to be there. I wanted it to be the way it had been when the Price family had been like my family and when it was a family that I thought would last forever. I could hear Bone breathing heavily above me so I lifted up my hand, seeking hers for comfort. She was a lifeline I needed very much at that moment. Somehow she understood and she took my hand in hers. She held it there for a very long time, a quiet comfort amidst the emotional storm I was weathering.

She spoke finally, softly, her voice low. "We'll find her, Denni. I know you and I deal in a world where little girls don't always come home safe and sound. But this is Kissy. Kissy. She's one strong little girl. She'll fight, Denni, and when she does we'll be here for her. Waiting, watching."

She crouched down and found my face with her hands. "We owe this to her, Denni. To not give up. If she fights, we fight. It's that simple and that direct."

I pondered her words and knew that I had it in me to find her. To search until I really, physically, could not search any more. I would mourn the dissolution of the strong Price family later, when I was alone and had the luxury of time to squander.

I mopped at my face with my shirtsleeves. "You're right. Of course. You're right, my smart, sensible Bone."

Struggling to my feet, I took Bone's hand, leading her farther up the hill where the going was smoother. Topping the incline, I realized that dawn was imminent; there was a subtle lightening of the sky along the horizon. Taking in a deep breath, I held it a long beat then exhaled slowly. Come on, Megs, help me out here, I thought. Your family needs you now more than ever before.

"Hey, Denni?" Bone tugged at my shoulder.

"Mmm?" I looked back toward the house. Flashlights peppered the fields below us like a swarm of fireflies.

"I saw a light," she said.

"I see lots of lights, honey," I replied absently. I was trying to decide our next move.

"Not over there, you don't."

I swiveled to face her, and my eyes followed her gaze. There, on the other side of the tributary, sure enough, there was a faint glow, bright because it was in the midst of an ebony darkness.

"What's over there?" I mused, searching my memory. Nothing would come.

"Turn off your light," Bone ordered in a low whisper. I complied and we were surrounded by an immense mantle of night. We stood very still, waiting for our eyes to adjust. The distant light wavered a bit, then moved slowly to the right. Then suddenly it was gone.

"We have to go, don't we?" Bone said, a small tremor in her voice.

"I think so," I said.

"Call Seychelles," she said.

I hesitated, my hand in my pocket on my cell. "Let's see what it is first. If it's a ghost, I don't want to give him a new story to share around the watercooler. Besides…I'm turned around and not exactly sure I could tell him where we are."

DAY SIX

CHAPTER THIRTY-FOUR

We inched our way down the incline, back the way we'd come. We were slow and methodical, depending on our other senses just as much as on sight. When we reached the water's edge, Bone tossed a small rock into the center. Then another.

"It's shallow," she determined. Taking my hand, she led the way across the slippery stones. Gaining the bank on the other side, we came up against what appeared to be a fence. I wanted to shine my light on it, but Bone warned me against it. In case it was electrified, I threw a handful of grass and dirt at it. Nothing sparked, so I felt confident enough to touch it gingerly with a fingertip. It was barbed wire only. I held the top strand up so Bone could wriggle through and she did the same for me. As we stood, we saw, by the lightening sky, an angled hill filled with grazing land that stretched as far as we could see. White sheep clumped together at one end of the field.

"I bet this is Taylor's land," I said. "I just knew that snake was involved somehow."

Bone stood next to me, trying to catch her breath in the humid heat released by the heavy plant growth around us. "There it is," she said urgently.

Off to our right there stood a large two-story barn, still a dark, lurking hulk in the morning dimness but a barn without doubt. And, visible through one of the windows—the one facing away from Fortune Farm—there shone a faint light. The barn was surrounded by large boxy-looking things. As we got closer, I realized they were old hay wagons, still piled with hay, that had been parked there along the barn walls.

Bone and I made our way cautiously along the fence line until we came upon the back of the huge barn. We heard indistinct voices from inside, then, like a knife in my heart, we heard a small child cry out. I wanted to go get her right away, but Bone wisely held me back.

"Why would Taylor take the child?" Bone asked.

"To blackmail John Clyde and make him sell the land so Taylor can buy it...for the oil," I whispered back.

"Ahhh," she sighed. "We need backup."

We crept to one of the back windows, only to find it so dirty that we couldn't see through it.

"Damn," I muttered. "We gotta go in, Bone. We need to get her out of there."

Bone sighed and reached to unholster her gun. I pulled mine out as well. Guns held high and ready, we moved around the back side of the barn and up the side. We passed a pale blue pickup, an older Ford model. I peered into the back and saw sawn boards piled haphazardly there, boards similar to the ones we'd found down at Ruddy Bayou. This was the same guy who had attacked her before.

We crept along slowly. The voices inside had faded, and so we were extra careful not to make any noise to alert Taylor to our presence. A shuffling sound came from inside, as though someone were climbing steps. Or maybe a ladder into the loft.

"I think he's up top," I whispered to Bone. She looked up, and I followed suit, not wanting someone to get the jump on us from above. The second-story doors were shut and latched as far as I could see. We moved on, over to the front door. I studied them. They were large, wide wooden plank doors, very old, and I knew the hinges would make a god-awful racket if I tried to open them all the way. Luckily the doors were parted and maybe, just maybe, if we were lucky, we could squeeze through and surprise him. I backed off to think it through. Would we be lucky?

Bone must have sensed my idea, because she nodded and started moving toward the opening. She slid through effortlessly, but I balked, knowing I would never fit without widening the opening. Bone nudged the door gently, and it silently moved a good three inches. Yes, we were lucky. I hitched my way through. Inside, there was nothing unusual, just a long hallway surrounded by open stalls on either side. The structure looked as though it hadn't been used in a while, and the smell of kerosene and old metal machinery was strong. We stood just inside the door, listening keenly for any sound. And then we heard it, a low musical humming. In a man's voice. The song was a familiar country one that I couldn't remember the name of, and I gripped my gun more tightly as a form began descending the ladder from the loft.

We remained dead still as the man stepped onto the wood planking of the barn floor. He hitched his jeans farther up his slim waist, and then he looked up and saw us.

"Hello, Rainerd. Your sister is looking for you," I said with steely calm.

His eyes grew huge in his long, thin face. "What did you tell her?" he asked. "Where is she?"

I shook my head. "Where's the little girl?"

He hung his head. There was a long silence.

Just as I was going to demand he tell me the whereabouts of Kissy, he began speaking. "I wasn't gonna hurt her. I just want him to sell this place and take her to Nashville."

"Take who to Nashville? Kissy?" I was trying to make sense of his words.

"Rina." He lifted his head. "She's a helluva singer. And she plays guitar. Since we was little kids, she's always had this dream of going to Nashville and being discovered. I believe that. I know she would...if she could just get there."

"What's holding her back, Rainerd?" Bone asked. She was in the shadows behind me, gun still aimed on him.

He shot her an angry glance before lowering his head again. "Me, I guess. But that's why I'm trying to fix things for her. To pay her back for looking after me all those years I was in jail and in rehab. She deserves to have a good life. If John Clyde would agree to move off the land here, to sell it, then they'd have enough to live on while she was taking her demo around to all the studios. I know Taylor wants it and John Clyde said himself that farming the land wasn't a joy anymore because of that fake sister of his. He said they weren't family, weren't real, you know, like Rina and me are real."

"This idea will never work, Rainerd," I said calmly, reasonably. "John Clyde loves this farm. And he would never give it up and move away, and, call me crazy, but I think your sister is okay with that."

"Maybe your sister doesn't even have that dream anymore. You know we all change as we get older." Bone told him.

"No!" He exclaimed loudly. "She needs to be a star. She deserves it. When I think of what she has given up...our mother was an alcoholic, a mean bitch, and when her liver started to go, Rina gave up on that dream, even though she had a chance, because she knew Mama needed her. And then when Mama died..."

"Then she had to take care of you," Bone added.

"Yes. So you see why I gotta give her this chance. She loves him, but I don't want her to give up again. And I'm gonna make sure she don't." His lip protruded like that of a petulant child. Indeed, that's what he seemed like to me, a young man with arrested development. He certainly did not seem to understand how wrong his actions were. And how much was at stake.

"Did you talk any of this over with Rina, Rainerd? Does she know what you are doing?" Bone said.

"No." His head snapped up. "And I don't want her to know."

"Too late," I muttered. "Now, where is the child?"

His demeanor changed in a heartbeat. "What did you tell her, you bitch?" He started moving toward me.

"Stop or I *will* take you down," I said firmly, readying my pistol.

He stopped in his tracks and stared me down.

"You'll have to tie him, Bone," I said. "We don't have cuffs."

"No problem," Bone replied. She holstered her gun and searched until she found an old horse cinch. "This should do," she said. She walked toward him, straightening and smoothing the leather strap in her hands. She began speaking as she approached him.

"Rainerd Beaudreaux, you are under arrest for the willful abduction of a child, holding her against her will, and for several counts of malicious destruction of property. You are also charged with bearing false witness against John Clyde Price and conspiring to destroy his life and livelihood. Please be advised that you have the right to remain silent and that anything you do say will be used against you in a court of law. You have the right to consult with an attorney and to have that attorney present during any questioning, and if you need an attorney, one will be provided at no cost to you. Do you understand these rights as I have told them to you?"

Just as she reached for him, his right hand shot out, there was a whistling noise and I felt a burning pain in my upper thigh. I looked down and saw a long metal blade protruding from my leg. My jeans began soaking up blood. I heard a scuffling sound and looked up. Rainerd had one arm wrapped around Bone's neck and was trying to get her gun. She was a smart girl and kept arcing her butt up toward him so he had no easy access to her back waistband. Not while he was holding her anyway. I steadied my gun and tried to get a shot at Rainerd around Bone.

She realized what I was trying to do, so with a quick nod, she dropped like a stone. Caught unawares, Rainerd couldn't catch her in time. I aimed in a split second and shot, the bullet catching him high in his right shoulder and spinning him around. Within seconds, he had disappeared into one of the stalls, but Bone was right on his heels.

I limped over, hissing at the jarring in my thigh as the knife moved. Bone had tackled him, and they were grappling in the cramped confines of what was essentially a small wooden box. He was trying to get her gun again, and so was she. His blood was everywhere, but she was holding her own against him. I tried to get another shot, but it was impossible; hay and blood were obscuring everything.

I backed off, holstered my gun and, reaching down, gingerly examined my leg. The knife had penetrated on the far outside, so I felt confident no artery had been compromised. There was an awful lot of blood, but that could be due to my racing heart. Bracing myself and gritting my teeth, I jerked the knife from my muscle. Using the bloody knife to start the rip, I tore off the bottom hem of my T-shirt and tied it tight around the wound. It hurt at first, then felt a little better. Certainly more secure.

"Bring him out here, I can't get him," I called over the noise of their scuffling and grunting. I stepped into the stall and tried to get a grip on him. It took about half a minute, but we were able to pull him out of the stall and into the walkway. He and Bone were both panting, beaten and bruised, and covered in bloody hay. Rainerd growled and slipped from our grip, shoving me into the edge of the opposite stall. I felt a crack as my back popped and I fell forward. Bone tried to trip him as he ran away, but though he stumbled, he didn't fall.

Suddenly I heard a faint cry, and I realized Kissy was up in the loft. "Let him go," I gasped. "Let's get Kissy and get the hell out of here. The cops will get him."

"Like hell they will!" She studied my face, her gaze dropping to my thigh. "Are you okay?"

I nodded. "I'll get her."

Bone disappeared, and I limped over to the ladder. Using my good leg, I put my foot on the first rung and lifted my weight. I had to use my wounded leg then, and using those thigh muscles was a new level of hell. I persevered, though, slowly, inch by inch, until my head was above the loft level. I saw Kissy then. She was lying on her side with her feet bound and her hands duct taped behind her back. Her mouth was taped as well, and her frightened eyes spoke volumes to me as I tried to figure out how I was going to get to her with my wounded leg. I pulled myself up one more rung and had to cry out from the pain of it. My leg throbbed now, even when my weight wasn't on it.

As if sensing my dilemma, Kissy started slithering and rolling across the floor to me.

"That's it, baby. Come over here so I can get the tape loose," I said, nodding vigorously. "I won't let you fall."

It seemed to take eons for her to get across the wide loft floor, and my mind was tortured worrying about Bone. I couldn't tell where they were or what was happening, and the lack of knowledge was killing me. I tried not to think about that, though, but tried to reassure Kissy with my eyes and my voice.

"Get back here, you bastard," Bone yelled. It came from my right, from the forested area. Obviously Rainerd was going to try and escape in the thick tree growth along the tributary.

"That's a brave girl, Katherine Grace. You just wait 'til I tell your mommies about what a brave girl you are. They are gonna be so proud of their girl," I told her, trying to make my voice strong.

Suddenly I smelled smoke. I twisted and looked below me and saw a most horrific sight. Rainerd was back in the barn and he was lighting hay on fire with a lighter. He looked up at me, panting heavily, and his eyes gleamed with hatred. "You took my sister from me," he spat out. "I hope you rot in hell."

He kicked over a large can of kerosene, and I wasted precious seconds watching in horror as the fluid snaked toward the fire. "Kissy, move faster, baby. Move faster!"

She reached me finally, and, after removing her gag, I tried to tear the thickly twisted duct tape binding her hands, but it was proving an impossible task. I thought about just carrying her down the ladder still bound but worried my bleeding leg wouldn't support her dead weight and my own and we'd fall into the fire. Suddenly a lightbulb flashed in my head, and I remembered the blade in the back pocket of my jeans. I had placed it there absently while binding my leg. I reached back and pulled it free and sliced through the tape that was holding Kissy's wrists. She cried out in pain as the binding came free and blood flooded into her extremities. I cooed reassuring inanities to her as I tried to plan our escape down the ladder. Looking down, I saw another sight that curdled my blood. Rainerd was preparing to mount the ladder. There was a look on his face that I wanted to forget as soon as I saw it. The man had certainly gone insane, and I knew in that moment that he was capable of murder. Smoke billowed up behind him, and I saw the first tentative lickings of flame.

I was paralyzed with fear, literally unable to move. I tried to suck in air, but even that wasn't going too well. I shut my eyes briefly and prayed for strength. I knew in that moment what I had to do.

"Back, Kissy, baby, move back, now!" I cried out.

Kissy scrambled back, crab walking across the rough, hay-strewn floor.

Using every bit of reserve I had in me, I hoisted my weight up the last two rungs and knelt on the loft floor. I screamed in agony. Gaining my feet, I threw an armful of hay and dust into Rainerd's face as it came over the edge of the loft. Then I spun, and, grabbing Kissy's hand, pulled her to her feet and toward the wide second-floor doors. Scrambling, my hands fumbling numbly, I released the latch just as a gunshot sounded. Oh my god, was he shooting at us?

I searched the ground below in the slanting, growing sunlight. There was a full hay trailer below the door, but it was not directly below and there was a chance we could not leap far enough. As I contemplated possibilities, I heard a voice calling from below.

"Denni? Denni, where are you?" It was Bone, and she was trying to breathe in and coughing in the same smoke that was billowing out of the upper doors around Kissy and me, choking us.

"Bone! Get out...there's kerosene! Get out," I yelled. "Get out...we're jumping." As I finished the warning a small explosion rocked the barn as if there had been a huge earthquake. The timbers groaned and a horrible smell filled my nostrils, threatening to smother me.

I grabbed Kissy up without thinking more about it, held her tiny body close to mine and launched us both into the morning sky.

CHAPTER THIRTY-FIVE

The hospital was a noisy place with a cacophony of squeaking shoes, odd beeps, patients crying out in pain and doors constantly whooshing open. I opened my eyes and sighed as the pain medication kicked in. It was about time. My small room was deserted, and so I let the tears fall unabated. Some were self-pity, I admit. I had been *that close* to finding love again, and then she was ripped from me. I was angry at the universe. Angry at all that was holy. I wanted to become an atheist. I *was* an atheist for a few moments. I saw Bone's beautiful, fragile face in my mind. I felt her slimness under my hands, and I cried ever harder, sobbing into my pillow.

How could life have dealt me this blow? Was I so undeserving? My thigh hurt, my back hurt, my spirit hurt. I could find no joy in the fact of Kissy's rescue. The fact that we had hit the wagon and emerged unscathed, except for a few cuts and bruises, that alone was nearly miraculous, but I no longer believed in miracles. I wept for what seemed like hours, and when I could cry no more, I fell into a deep, drugged sleep.

I woke sometime later, my mouth cottony and a warm, slim arm wrapped around me. I enjoyed that dream state for a moment, then blinked open my thick eyes and stared at the window. My head felt numb, sinuses heavy from crying. I moved to turn over and a startled cry paralyzed me.

"Ow, damn it, that hurts!" Bone said next to my ear. "Give a gal some warning, why dontcha?"

Heart soaring, I painfully moved back, turning my body over so I could look at her, could verify that it was really her. Yes, it was Bone. Broken, bruised, scraped, but my Bone. New tears welled in my eyes and spilled out to run down and tickle my ears. Bone watched me with those laughing blue eyes.

"Just stop that, you silly goose," she said, leaning to lovingly kiss them away. She leaned back to study me. "The doc says you're okay. It's just a flesh wound, a deep one, but they've packed it and bandaged it and they're gonna let it heal from the inside out."

"And you? I was sure the explosion had killed you."

"Nope, I was running out, thanks to you, and was blown into the trees. That's how I broke this." She indicated her arm. I now saw that it was in a bright green cast and cradled in a dark blue sling. That's what must have hurt when I rolled over on her. I smiled. Hell, I bet everything both of us had would hurt for a while.

"Oh, you think that's funny," Bone asked, her expression astonished.

I laughed and caressed her thigh. "No, babe, I was just thinking about what a long strange week we've had."

She sighed and shifted to get more comfortable on the narrow hospital bed. "You can say that again. This won't be one vacation I forget anytime soon."

I watched her, adoring her sweet face, even scraped and spotted with purpling bruises as it was. Even her bottom lip was busted. "No, I won't let you forget it. I'll be there every day as a constant reminder."

She smiled and kissed the tip of my nose. "You will, huh? You moving to Richmond?"

"You never know," I replied. "You never know."

"Hey, what happened to Rainerd after I threw stuff at him?" I asked after some minutes had passed. "Did he die in the explosion?"

Bone grimaced and shut her eyes as if pained. "No, I shot him when he was up on the ladder. He won't bother the Price family ever again."

* * *

They released us later that evening, and Patty came back to the hospital to pick us up. Kissy had been examined earlier and, as she had not been harmed in any significant way, had been allowed to go home at lunchtime. They'd kept Bone and me a little longer.

As we made our slow way to the kitchen door, John Clyde and Erica came out to greet us.

"Denni, Bone, I'm sorry," he said as he held the door for us. "I was so wrong to react that way."

I nodded and maneuvered my crutches around so I could look at him. So I could stare at him a long time, even though I was making Patty and Bone wait behind me. "Are you grown up now?"

He hung his head in shame. "Yeah."

"He'd better be," Erica said, giving me a warm hug and a kiss on the cheek. "I have a direct line to Megs, and I'm gonna keep him in line for her."

Patty paused and gave Erica a big hug before passing through the doorway. I looked back to see how John Clyde had reacted to it. He was watching with tolerance, if not outright approval.

Ammie met us in the kitchen, and she pulled me close, her arms trembling. She pulled back and looked at me but was so emotionally wrought that she couldn't speak. I patted her cheek with one hand.

"Man, something smells good!" I said, looking around the kitchen, hoping to give her time to get her emotions under control.

"It's your favorite," Yolanda said, striding into the kitchen, Kissy on her heels.

"Mine too," Kissy added. "Macaroni and cheese!"

She raced forward and wrapped her arms around my legs, pressing her cheek firmly to my belly. "Thank you *so* much for coming to get me, Denni," she said. "MomPatty told MomLanda I'd be dead if you hadn't come to get me and pulled me out of that barn."

I smiled and caressed her tousled curls. "I don't know about all that, but I do know I was mighty glad to see you when I did."

I turned to Patty as Kissy ran into the dining room. "Was Taylor involved? Was he working with Rainerd?" I asked quietly. "He was in his barn."

She shook her head. "No. Rainerd was on his own. Taylor just wanted to buy us out and John Clyde was putting him off. Seems John Clyde had a suspicion about the oil. He's been testing the land for months. So when we called Taylor and told him what happened to his barn, he was okay about it. We're gonna help him rebuild it, even though he doesn't want us to."

"So Rainerd did all this…just so Rina could have a music career?" Bone asked, looking into some of the open pots on the stove and peering in the oven door. She must have been hungry. I smiled as I watched her.

Patty nudged me playfully. "Yep, that's why. Though John Clyde says she gave up on that dream a long time ago and has no plans to pursue it."

"She might just want to be a farmer's wife," John Clyde added, smiling a big goofy grin.

Ammie groaned low in her throat. "Oh lordy! Look, let's get you all fed," she continued briskly. "I know hospital food wouldn't keep a bird alive. Y'all go on in and set yourselves down. Buster's already in there, reading the paper so y'all act proper now. Don't embarrass me."

I looked at Bone. "Buster?" I mouthed. She shrugged.

We moved *en masse* into the dining room. Sure enough, Officer Seychelles was sitting in the middle of one side of the table, a newspaper open on the polished surface before him.

"Well, look what the cat done drug in," he said, laughing in a low chuckle. "Y'all are certainly a sight to see. I am so glad none of y'all winded up dead. The paperwork woulda kept me busy for days."

John Clyde groaned at the poor joke and sobered. "Yeah, we were lucky. Rina not so much."

We fell silent, thinking about her loss.

"He had a death wish," I said finally. "Otherwise he would have gotten out of the barn before it exploded. That, or he was just so mad at me, at us, that he plain didn't realize. Maybe he wasn't thinking right."

"Rina says he's been in trouble off and on his whole life," John Clyde said. "You ever think that just some people are born bad? I actually think she might be just a little relieved to not have to deal with any more of his crap."

The doorbell rang and John Clyde moved into the foyer. "Speak of the devil," he muttered.

Moments later, he was back with Rina. This was the first time I'd seen her in regular clothing, and she did look fetching in her jeans and blouse. I could tell she was upset, that she had been crying. But I could also see an air of fatalistic acceptance about her. She'd be all right. She handed a small paper bag to John Clyde. "This was all they had left," she said. "It's mostly there."

John Clyde kissed Rina's cheek and handed the bag to Patty.

"Mama's jewelry," he said, his eyes lowered. "What they didn't sell."

He stood, head bowed, as Patty upended the bag into one palm. Megs's pearls spilled out, followed by her wedding band set and several brooches that I remembered her wearing.

Patty, eyes gleaming, looked up at her brother. I think words failed her. She opened her mouth a time or two but said nothing. Finally, her fingers curled around the jewelry and she pulled him close.

I had to look away from the tender scene as my eyes filled. I heard a few suspicious sniffles behind me.

After some time, John Clyde took Patty's hand and led her to the table.

"Sorry I'm so late," Rina said as she mopped her eyes with a tissue. "I hope I didn't hold up dinner."

John Clyde ushered her to a seat, as Patty reached over and patted her hand. "Not a bit, sweetness, not a bit," she said. "Now that everyone's here, Kissy, will you say grace for us?"

Kissy's prayer was long, rambling and heartfelt as she gave thanks for several members of the police force for keeping her warm with blankets after the fire and for me, because I had rescued her from the fire. She did not mention anything about the bad man, Rainerd, and I thought that was pretty astute for a four-year-old.

After the prayer finished, I noticed that there was a worn leather book, a journal, in the center of the table, dishes of food reverently surrounding it as Ammie and Erica brought them in. I knew immediately what it was, and tears welled in my eyes anew. Patty had laid Megs's jewelry on top.

"Denni, we sure are gonna miss you and Bone when you fly off tomorrow," Patty said as she dished up salad and passed the bowls along the table.

"I don't think I'll miss being here much," I joked as I dabbed at my eyes. "At least in Virginia no one expects to be rescued. And I don't have to jump from burning barns on a regular basis."

"Yet," John Clyde added.

The entire table joined in the laughter, and I began to sense the extent of the healing that had come over Fortune Farm. I looked at the beloved faces around the table—Megs in the center, then Kissy, Patty, Yolanda, Officer Seychelles, Rina and John Clyde. And seated on the other side were Erica, Ammie, Bone and me. A perfect family.

DAY SEVEN

CHAPTER THIRTY-SIX

The Lake Charles airport seemed to be asleep early Saturday morning when Patty parked in front of it. We'd said our goodbyes to everyone else back at the house, and I had, packed in my carry-on, a full basket of fresh strawberries, Ammie's payment to me for vanquishing the evil that had befallen the family. I wasn't quite sure how I would get them through security, but Bone promised that as a cop, she'd get them through or we would eat them...very fast.

I glanced over and watched Bone as she hugged Yolanda and Patty, saying further farewells. God, she was a gorgeous woman. I was very proud to be flying back to Virginia with her as my love. We had already gone online and changed our seats so we could sit next to one another, and I was looking forward to the time alone with her in the cocoon of an airplane. In addition, we could help one another navigate airports—her with a broken arm and me still on crutches. We *were* the walking wounded. I didn't mind at all. It could have been a whole lot worse.

Then Patty was standing before me. "You guys gonna be okay from here, or do you need us to help you inside?"

"No, we're good. Give Kissy and Ammie each one more kiss from me, okay?"

"I sure am gonna miss you," she said as I drew her into my arms. "I'm glad we're friends," she added against my ear. I nodded, feeling tears well and not trusting my voice to speak.

Yolanda came over and pulled me into a big hug, tighter than I would have expected. "Thank you for saving our baby," she said. "I can never repay you, just know you will always have a home with us. You hear me?" She speared me with a hawk-like glance and I smiled widely. Now that's what I'm talking about, I thought. Maybe there *was* more to Landa than met the eye.

I held her shoulder and nodded as I returned her look. "You take care of that family, now. I'll be checking in by email and phone," I said with an elbow shove so she'd know I wasn't criticizing in any way.

"Hey, Denni, did you hear about the oil?" Patty called as she was preparing to get into her car.

"No, what about it?"

"Instead of selling out to Taylor, John Clyde and me are gonna arrange to have some wells put in down in Southland. We're gonna be rich." She and Yolanda looked at one another and broke into spontaneous laughter. They were still guffawing as they got into the car and drove away.

"You already are," I whispered to the disappearing vehicle.

"Indeed," Bone said at my side.

I turned to Bone and stared into her eyes, losing myself in their mesmerizing depths. "Hey, you remember that decision I told you that I had made? Whether to get on with my life or simply decide I couldn't live without Patty?"

"Yes. Yes, I do. And what did you decide?" she asked, tilting her head to one side in that adorable way she had.

"I've decided to get on with my life. I've decided to choose you," I said, taking her uninjured hand and pressing the palm to my lips. She moved her fingers in a soft caress of my cheek.

Bone and I continued to look at one another, heat and electricity passing between us. We lingered in the glow for a long moment, then we smiled and, carefully hoisting our carry-on bags, walked into the quiet airport. Together.

Bella Books, Inc.

Women. Books. Even Better Together.

P.O. Box 10543
Tallahassee, FL 32302

Phone: 800-729-4992
www.bellabooks.com